THE GREATEST
GIFT

LARRY
BUTTRAM

Larry Buttram

www.larrybuttram.com

Published in the United States by:
New Virginia Publications
9185 Matthew Dr.
Manassas Park, Va. 20111

SAN 256-0453

First Printing - August, 2006

Book Cover and Layout by Allison Media
www.allisonmedia.com

ISBN 978-0-9755030-5-7
ISBN 0-975503057
LCCN 2006927449

www.LarryButtram.com

CONTENTS

THE GREATEST GIFT

Set against a dreary, overcast, November sky, the aging, red-brick building stood alone in the parking lot. The gray sedan crept slowly toward the building, coming to a stop near the entrance. A small gloved hand rubbed the fog from the back window, allowing two curious eyes to examine the building. The man and woman exchanged a sad smile, then exited the car. The woman opened the rear door, allowing the young child to exit. The couple took the girl's hands and led her slowly to the building. They climbed the steps to the third floor and soon found the office for which they were searching. The sign on the door read *Greatest Gift Foundation.* The couple exchanged a quick glance, then led the child into the room.

The waiting room was as austere as the exterior of the building. The only furnishings were a couch, three chairs, and a couple of end tables. Children's magazines were strewn haphazardly across the tables. The child had only begun to examine a magazine when the door to the adjoining office opened. In walked a slender, balding, black man in his early thirties. He smiled and greeted the visitors. "Mr. and Mrs. Renner, I'm Jack Ellis," he said as he shook their hands. "Won't you and your daughter please come into my office?"

The family followed him into the room. Mr. Ellis sat behind an ancient but well preserved oak desk, his visitors taking a seat facing him. Once seated, he continued. "I know this is a difficult time for all of you. I just hope we can make it a little more bearable."

The couple thanked him politely. He then turned to the child. "And you're Stephanie, who I've heard so much about."

"Yes, sir," she responded.

"That's a very nice name. I've always liked it," he said.

"Thank you," she replied with a warm smile.

"Did you have a nice Thanksgiving, Stephanie?"

"It was very nice, thank you. Did you?"

"Why, yes, I did," he returned with a slight laugh. "How nice of you to ask."

He glanced at the couple for assurance before continuing. They both sat emotionless. He turned back to the child. "Do you know why you're here, Stephanie?" he asked.

"Yes, of course. I'm going to die and you're going to grant me my last wish. You don't have to be afraid to talk about it."

He looked up at the parents, then smiled at Stephanie. It always made it a little more bearable when the child had come to terms with their illness. Even so, it was never easy.

"Fine, Stephanie," he said warmly. "I hope you've given some thought to your wish. And don't be afraid to ask for something difficult. We've taken little girls to meet their favorite actor or actress; we've had little boys meet their sports hero; we've taken children to Disney World; why, we've even had a couple of kids meet the President."

"I already know what my wish is," she said.

"Well, great. Just tell me what you want and we'll do our best to provide it."

"I need to go to the top of Mt. Everest."

"Mt. Everest?" repeated Mr. Ellis.

"Yes," she continued, "that's the tallest mountain in the world, isn't it?"

He looked at the parents for an explanation.

"That's all she's been talking about for weeks," said her mother. "We've already tried to talk to her, but nothing is impossible to a six-year-old."

Mr. Ellis turned back to the child. "Yes, Stephanie, it is the tallest mountain in the world, but why would you want to go there?"

"So I can talk to Jesus," she answered quickly.

"And what would you say to Jesus?"

"I would tell Him to talk to all the other little boys and girls in the world who are dying, so that they don't have to be afraid. I would tell Him that He has to let them know that when they die they're just going home to be with Him."

Her mother took her handkerchief and wiped away her tears, as her father closed his eyes and took a deep breath. Jack Ellis thought, after five years in the job, that no request could surprise him. He was wrong. He quickly tried to think of a way to respond to such an impossible wish.

"Well, Stephanie, I believe in Jesus, too. But, if you believe in Him, you must know that He's everywhere. Why would you have to go to the top of a mountain to talk to Him?"

"Don't you understand?" she said sternly. "Everyone is talking to Him. He can't hear just me. If He did then He would talk to all the other kids like me and they wouldn't be so scared. I have to be at the top of the mountain so I'm the closest to heaven."

"But Stephanie," he continued, "Jesus hears all the little kids' prayers."

"Mr. Ellis, do you mean that Jesus heard me ask Him to talk to all the other sick kids in the world and He still won't do it?"

"Well, honey, I don't think it's quite that simple. The kids have to want to listen to Jesus also."

"But why wouldn't any kid want to listen to Him if He was telling them that they're going to heaven?"

Mr. Ellis looked to her parents for assistance.

"She asks some pretty tough questions for a six-year-old, doesn't she?" asked her father.

The mother took her handkerchief away from her eyes and spoke. "Since she was a toddler we've had her in Sunday school to learn about God, but now I'm not sure how to answer her questions."

Jack Ellis turned back to Stephanie, still searching for the right words to say. "Stephanie, honey," he began, "do you know that only a few people have ever been to Mt. Everest?"

"Yes, my daddy told me that."

"And did you know that no child has ever been there?"

"Yes."

"Then, honey, you must know that, as much as I want to grant your wish, it's just impossible."

"Mrs. Franklin told me that if a person really believes in something and trusts in Jesus, nothing is impossible."

He gave a questioning look to her parents.

"Mrs. Franklin was her Sunday school teacher," said her father.

"She died this year, too," said Stephanie.

The three adults stared at each other at the finality of her statement. Mr. Ellis turned back to the child. "But, Stephanie, honey, isn't there something else you would like for us to do for you?"

"No thank you," she responded politely. "I just have to do this for all the other sick children."

He looked at her for a second, took a deep breath, and leaned back in his seat.

"Okay, honey," he continued. "I can't promise you anything, but I'll do everything I can to grant you your wish. Now, can you wait in the other room for just a minute while I talk to your parents?"

"Yes, sir," she said as she arose. "And thank you, Mr. Ellis. I told my parents you'd understand."

She left the room, leaving the adults staring at one another. After a few seconds Mr. Ellis spoke. "Do you think there's a possibility she might change her mind about this?"

"No, I don't," answered Mrs. Renner. "She saw a show on TV about terminally ill children a few weeks ago, and she's talked about nothing else since. I believe this is her way of doing something to be remembered by."

"She seems to have come to terms with her situation pretty well."

"I guess so," said Mrs. Renner. "It was really tough for her in the beginning, but I guess she's in the final stage - what do they call it - resolution?"

Mr. Ellis only shook his head. "Well," he continued, "if I may ask one more question - why doesn't she wait until she's - uh, until she can talk to Jesus in person to tell Him this?"

"You mean when she gets to heaven?" she clarified.

"Yes."

"She says she won't remember."

"Won't remember?"

"Yes. She says if she remembered all the sick children it would make her sad, and there's no sadness in heaven, so she won't remember."

"Wow," he responded.

Mr. Ellis turned to Mr. Renner. He had seen the look before - a look of sadness, helplessness, and anger. He was almost afraid to ask for his comments but felt he had to do so.

"Mr. Renner," he asked, "do you have any suggestions?"

"Do I have any suggestions?" he repeated sarcastically. "No, I don't have any suggestions. I just think it's pretty ironic that she wants to go talk to a God that would tear a beautiful little six-year-old girl away from her parents. It's just not fair."

"No, it isn't," he responded as his eyes dropped to the floor. "And, as many times as I've been through this you would think I would have the answer but I don't. As I said, I'm a Christian also, but there are still many things I don't understand. All I can say is that I'm sorry."

After a few seconds of silence Mrs. Renner spoke. "Mr. Ellis, we've already told Stephanie that her request would be impossible so don't be too worried about it. We'll talk to her again and see if we can get her to settle for something more reasonable."

"Before you do that, Mrs. Renner, how about giving me a few days to see what I can do?"

"We appreciate your concern, Mr. Ellis," said Mr. Renner, "but we both know her request is impossible."

"That's true, at least as far as Mt. Everest is concerned, but maybe I can come up with an alternative she will feel meets her needs. I would at least like a little time to work on it. I hate to ask you this, but...well...how long..?"

"She saw the doctor just a few days before Thanksgiving and he estimates a couple of months, maybe less," said Mrs. Renner through her tears.

"Well, maybe I can come up with a solution and we can set something up before Christmas. Just don't give up hope yet."

He thanked the couple for coming and walked them to the door. He felt a tremendous sadness - worse than he could remember since being in the job - as he watched them walk away. With all his heart he wished he had an explanation as to why their little girl had to die. He had none. All he could hope for was to find a way to satisfy her last request.

The trip from Pittsburgh to their home in Washington, Pennsylvania took less than an hour. By the time they arrived back home, Stephanie had fallen asleep. Her father gently lifted her and carried her to her bed. After covering her with her favorite blanket, he returned to the living room and sat on the couch, his face buried in his hands. His wife sat beside him, gently rubbing his shoulders.

"Will, Are you okay?" she asked.

"I don't think I'll ever be okay again," he answered. "I don't see how, if there really is a God, that He could let something like this happen. She's about the most perfect little girl that ever lived."

"Honey, please don't say something like that. We don't know God's plans. We can only see things from our perspective. You can't let this destroy your faith in God."

"I'm serious, Liz," he answered as he turned to her. "I'm not even sure I believe in God anymore. I've spent a lot of time thinking about this, and it's just very difficult for me to accept an all-powerful and all-loving God that allows something like this to happen to a little girl. I know we hear about terrible things happening all over the world, but it really doesn't mean anything until it happens to you.

"Honey," she continued, "why do you have to try and make sense out of everything? It's bad enough to have to deal with this without driving yourself insane trying to understand it."

"I have to understand it, Liz, or else I can never accept it. I just can't accept something on faith like you can. If there is a God, then there has to be a reason why things like this are allowed to happen."

"I don't know, Will," she said wearily, "perhaps there's a reason for this. Perhaps - although we can't see it now - there will be a greater good that comes from Stephanie's death."

"So now you're saying that you believe in a God who would sacrifice a little girl just to make a point? I can't accept that."

She put her hands in her lap and leaned back on the couch. She looked at her husband, took a deep breath, and spoke softly. "Then maybe God has nothing to do with this. Maybe He just created the world and put it in motion and doesn't interfere anymore. I don't have the answers for you, Will. I just know your little girl knows she's going to heaven, so I hope you don't let her see your doubts."

"I would never do that," he answered quickly.

They sat silently for a moment before Will rose from the couch and walked to the bedroom where his daughter was sleeping. He watched her for a few seconds before moving quietly to the bed. He gently lay down beside her, placed his arm over her, and soon fell asleep.

Five days passed before the Renner family heard from Jack Ellis. Although her parents tried to explain that her wish may be impossible to grant, Stephanie was confident that Mr. Ellis would find a way. When he identified himself to Mrs. Renner on the phone, she was sure he was calling to offer his apologizes. Her eyes widened when he informed her that he wished to meet with them to discuss granting Stephanie's wish.

"You've got to be joking," she said. "We all know that there's no way humanly possible to take a little girl to the top of Mt. Everest."

"Of course not," he responded, "but climbing the mountain is just a means to an end for her. I believe I have a solution to her real request."

"What do you mean?"

"That's why I want to come over," he answered. "I would like to talk to all three of you together. Can I come by and meet with you soon?"

"Okay," she said, still confused.

They agreed for him to come by the following evening.

It was just after dinner when Jack Ellis arrived at the Renners' house. Stephanie hurried to the door to greet their visitor. She did, however, wait until they were seated to begin her questioning.

"So, are you going to take me to Mt. Everest?" she asked.

"Well," he began with a laugh, "no, but I believe I did find a way to grant you your wish."

"What do you mean?" she asked. "I have to go to Mt. Everest."

"Stephanie," he began as he leaned forward, "didn't you tell me that the reason you want to go to Mt. Everest was so you could talk to Jesus?"

"Yes, so He'll tell all the other sick children to not be scared anymore."

"Well then, isn't that your real wish? Isn't going to the top of the mountain just a way to talk to Jesus?"

"Yes, but that's the only way."

"Well, what if there's another way - a better way? Would you agree to it?"

She looked at her father for an answer. He just shrugged his shoulders.

"I guess so," she answered.

"Well, I believe I have a better and much easier way for you to get your message to Jesus."

"How?" she demanded.

"Well, do you ever listen to the radio?"

"Of course, in my daddy's car."

"Well, there's a radio station in Chicago that is the biggest and most powerful station in the world. It sends out signals all over the world. It even sends radio signals tens of thousands of miles into space."

"Is that true, Daddy?" she asked cautiously.

"Well I'm sure it is if Mr. Ellis says so. Chicago is an awfully big city and they do have some big radio stations there."

"And guess what, Stephanie," Mr. Ellis continued.

"What?"

"I've talked to the owner and he says you can use the station to talk to Jesus. How does that sound?"

She looked at her parents for an answer.

"Mommy?"

"Honey, I think that's a great idea. It'll be much easier for Jesus to hear you from a radio station like that than it would be from the top of a mountain."

"And all the other sick children in the world will be able to hear you too," added her father. "And you know they wouldn't be able to hear you from the mountain."

"Hey, that's right," she said with a smile. She then turned back to Mr. Ellis. "When can we go to Chicago?"

"I thought we could do it Christmas day. How does that sound?"

"We can't do it on Christmas day," she stated.

"Why can't we do it Christmas day?" he asked as he looked at her parents. "I thought that would be the best time."

"Because that's when all the angels bring Jesus His birthday presents, silly. I don't want to bother Him then."

"Oh," he returned. "Why didn't I think of that? What about Christmas Eve?"

"That would be fine," she answered. "Will my Mommy and Daddy be able to go?"

"Of course. We wouldn't think of sending you without them."

"And will you be able to go, Mr. Ellis?"

"Certainly, that is, if it's okay with you."

"I would like that very much. You're a nice man."

She arose and gave him a hug. Tears came to his eyes as he held her close. After a second she moved back and said, "I'm kind of tired now, so I think I'll go to bed. Thank you for granting my wish, Mr. Ellis."

She smiled and left for her room. After a minute Mr. Renner spoke.

"Mr. Ellis, are you serious about this?"

"Absolutely."

"How could you arrange something like this so quickly?" asked Mr. Renner.

"Actually it wasn't that difficult. The station owner thought it was a great idea - to have a little girl talk to God on his station at Christmas. He said he was doing it because it was the right thing to do, but I'm sure he won't mind the publicity either."

Mr. Renner looked troubled.

"Is there something else you wanted to say?" asked Mr. Ellis.

"No - well yes, I guess there is. I hate to say this but, to tell you the truth, I'm just not sure she'll be able to make a trip like that by that time."

"We'll do everything we can to make it as easy on her as possible. It's only about an hour's flight and the airline donates first class accommodations. We'll have a car pick you up here and will have another one at the airport in Chicago. And we'll have a room for your family near the airport. We have much experience at this, Mr. Renner."

"I appreciate that, but..."

"That's fine, Mr. Ellis," interrupted his wife. "You've already made an agreement with Stephanie and we'll be there."

Mr. Renner turned to his wife as if to respond but, after looking into her eyes, dropped his head and nodded.

"Mr. Renner," said Mr. Ellis, "I wish there was something more I could do to make this easier, but I can't. All I can do again is say I'm sorry."

"You've done more than enough," said Mr. Renner, "and I do appreciate it. I'm just not too good at showing it right now."

He nodded his understanding as he arose. He placed his hand on Will Renner's shoulder for a second and walked to the door. They thanked him once more for his help. Mrs. Renner put her arm around her husband as they watched him walk to his car.

As Jack Ellis had promised, the airport limousine arrived at exactly four o'clock. The flight was scheduled to depart at five-forty-five, Eastern Time, arriving in Chicago at six o'clock Central Time. Stephanie's broadcast was to be at nine o'clock, which would give them enough time to check in at the hotel before leaving for the station. Stephanie had already rehearsed her speech, which was scheduled to last only five minutes. She had planned most of it herself, although frequently calling upon her parents for advice.

Due to a commitment in another city, Jack Ellis would not be making the trip with them but would be joining them at the radio station. He had, however, made all arrangements for their trip before his departure.

Mr. Renner had growing reservations about the trip. His

daughter's condition had gradually gotten worse, and she spent much of the day sleeping. Still, she never complained. In fact, the thing that brought her the most joy was her planned trip to talk to her friend, Jesus.

Mr. Renner also had concerns over the weather in the Chicago area. A winter storm watch was in effect for northern Illinois, although the forecasters were predicting only a couple of inches. The gloomy weather, coupled with his daughters worsening illness, created in him an overwhelming feeling of sadness.

As Jack Ellis had explained, the airline had reserved three first class seats for them, however, with only two adjoining seats, her father was forced to sit behind Stephanie. While the flight was only half full, he was soon interrupted by a passenger taking the adjoining seat. He was a small, rotund man who appeared to be in his early fifties.

"Excuse me," the man said with a warm smile as he waited to get by.

"Sure," said Mr. Renner dryly as he stood to allow the passenger to take his seat.

It was only a short time before the plane was airborne. A few minutes later, the flight attendant delivered their dinner. Stephanie took only a few bites before telling her mother she was full. The attendant returned shortly to take the tray. Once the tray was gone, she turned to her father to inform him that she was going to take a nap.

Mr. Renner's seatmate observed Stephanie for some time before speaking. "Is your daughter okay?" he asked.

Mr. Renner stared at him blankly before answering. At first he wanted to demand how he could ask such a question of a total stranger, but, for some unknown reason, he felt compelled to respond. "No, I'm sorry to say," he returned, "she's a very sick little girl."

"I'm terribly sorry to hear that," returned the stranger. "Are you taking her to Chicago for treatment?"

"No. She's going to be on a radio program tonight."

"Oh," he acknowledged, "then you're Mr. and Mrs. Renner?"

"How did you know that?"

"You've gotten a lot more publicity than you realize. At least Stephanie has."

"Oh, yeah," he said with a shake of the head as he thought of the newspaper articles written about the sick little girl who was going to talk to Jesus.

"It seems that Stephanie is dealing quite well with this," continued the stranger, "but how are you doing?"

"Look," said Mr. Renner, "I appreciate your concern, but I really don't want to talk about this."

"Forgive me for being so blunt," pursued the stranger, "but I sense you really do need to talk about it."

Mr. Renner looked at him in confusion and anger. He was irritated that a stranger would attempt to interfere in such a private and painful part of their life. But there was also something about him, a sense of compassion, that made him want to discuss the matter.

"Look, mister, the only thing I want to know is how God - if there really is one - can let something like this happen to such a sweet little girl. Can you answer that?"

Mrs. Renner turned to her husband as if to caution him, but then, after realizing her daughter was sleeping soundly, said nothing.

"Well, Mr. Renner," began the stranger, "I don't have all the answers, but I've given a lot of thought to your question in my life. Maybe I can help a little. Let me ask you a question. What exactly would you like God to do?"

"That's easy. Heal my daughter."

"That's quite understandable. Anyone in your position would want the same thing. But I now must ask you another question. If He did heal your daughter, should He also heal every other sick child in the world?"

"I don't know. I don't have answers to questions like that. All I know is that I want my daughter healed."

"But so do millions of other parents in the world. So the question remains, does God intervene to heal every sick child in the world?"

"I don't know?"

"And if he did, should He then also heal every sick adult in the world?"

"I told you, I don't have the answer to your question."

"And what about accidents? Does He prevent people from being killed in accidents? And how would He do that? Does He take control of their lives so they don't do anything stupid? Does He stop a child from running in front of a car? Does He change the course of a bullet?"

"Those are ridiculous questions. And I'm not sure what your intentions are but this isn't helping me."

"But I have a feeling that these are some of the questions you've been asking yourself for many weeks now. Why my daughter? How can this happen? Why is life so unfair? I think you are a lot like me. You have a difficult time accepting things on faith. You need a logical answer to why things happen. That's what I am trying to show you."

Mr. Renner turned away from the mysterious man. It was true - he had been thinking many of the things he had said. And the stranger had raised many valid points. If this were only a philosophical discussion, perhaps he would be more accepting, but it was not. His daughter's life was slowly slipping away, and he was still very angry. He soon turned back to the man.

"You seem to know a lot about God. Do you believe that God heals people?"

"Yes, I know He has that power."

"Then why doesn't He heal my daughter?"

"Mr. Renner, I'm sad to say I can't answer that question. I do believe that God can and does heal people, but, as I said, there are many things I don't understand. I don't know why some people are healed and some aren't. We can only look at things from the human level. We can only measure things in terms of our own suffering or happiness. But to God, perhaps a little girl dying and going to heaven is not a punishment."

Mr. Renner sat silently for a few minutes, contemplating what the man had said. Even though many of the things he'd said made sense, his words could not remove the hurt in his heart. "Well," he said slowly, "I appreciate your sharing your feelings with me. To be honest though, it doesn't make me feel a lot better. I think the greatest gift God can give is a little girl like we have, and now he's taking her away. It's not fair."

"Like I said, Mr. Renner," the man returned, "I don't have all the answers. I think all you can do is remember what God did and didn't promise. He created people and gave us our freedom to make our own decisions. Unfortunately we used our freedom to disobey Him. We wanted to be as knowledgeable and powerful as God. That's how sin - and with sin, death - entered the world. And, to take away our sin He sent His Son - a Son who also suffered and died for us. All we have to do is believe in Him to receive eternal life. When you think about it, that's really the only thing that God promised, and I believe He's kept that promise."

Mr. Renner was contemplating what the stranger had said. His thoughts were soon interrupted by the Captain's voice.

"Ladies and Gentlemen," he began, "it looks like we have a little bad news. The storm around Chicago has gotten much worse. They're closing the airport for a while so we're being diverted to the Champaign/Urbana airport. For those of you not familiar with the area, that's a little over 100 miles from Chicago. The storm line goes just south of Chicago so there will be no problem landing there. You can meet an airline representative when we land to discuss other transportation or accommodations. I'm sorry for the inconvenience but we really have no choice. Your safety is our first concern."

Mrs. Renner turned to look to her husband. He shook his head in disbelief.

"What now?" she asked.

"I don't know. I guess we can get a rental car. The radio station is south of the city, so according to what the pilot is saying, we shouldn't have any trouble getting there. And we should have plenty of time. We just won't be able to go to the hotel first."

The stranger leaned forward to speak.

"My sister is picking me up at the airport. I'm sure that when she heard that traffic was being diverted to Champaign, she'll meet me there. You're more than welcome to ride with us."

"That's very nice of you," said Mrs. Renner, "but I think she may be too late for us if she has to come all the way from Chicago."

"Well, she lives half way between the two, so it's only about forty-five minutes to each airport. She probably is already on her way. We should only have to wait a half hour at the most. And I'm sure you two probably don't even know the area, right?"

"That's true. If that's no trouble we would sure appreciate the help. I just hope she doesn't have any problem in all this snow," said Mr. Renner.

"I wouldn't worry about it. No matter what happens I'm sure you'll get to the station in time," returned the stranger.

Thirty minutes later the captain announced they were approaching the Champaign/Urbana airport. Because of the traffic being diverted from Chicago, they were forced to circle the field for fifteen minutes. They then waited another ten minutes for a gate to become available. It was six-forty-five when they finally exited the plane. Stephanie awoke as her father was picking her up. He explained that they had landed in another city and would have to drive to Chicago.

"Will we still make it to the radio station in time, Daddy?" she asked.

"Of course, honey," he assured her. She hugged his neck and put her head on his shoulder.

Stephanie informed her parents that she needed to use the bathroom. The man on the plane told them he too needed to stop at the bathroom. He told them he would meet them at the luggage area after he called his sister on her cell phone to make sure she was aware of the flight being redirected.

A few minutes later, Mrs. Renner exited from the bathroom

carrying her daughter. Stephanie stated that she could walk but her parents convinced her to save her energy for her radio broadcast.

They walked to the luggage area and claimed their suitcase. They scanned the area for their new friend but did not see him. Will Renner walked around the room but the stranger was nowhere in sight. He questioned a skycap who informed him that there was no other luggage area at the airport. They waited almost fifteen minutes before deciding to rent a car. Mrs. Renner asked her husband what could have happened to the mysterious stranger, but Will Renner only shook his head in disgust.

They soon made their way to the rental car counter, feeling lucky when they saw that no one was in line. They informed the young woman behind the counter that they needed a car to get to Chicago.

"I'm sorry," she informed them, "but we have absolutely no vehicles left. It's because of the storm and everyone being redirected here."

"But, Miss," pleaded Mr. Renner, "it's critical that we get to Chicago within two hours. You must have something."

"I'm terribly sorry, sir, but we have absolutely nothing, not even a van."

"What about the other rental companies - do you know if they have anything?"

"I just talked to them, and unfortunately they're in the same situation. There's not a vehicle left to rent anywhere at the airport."

"What about a shuttle or limo? Is there such a thing from here to Chicago?"

"Yes, there's a shuttle, but it just left. There won't be another one for another hour."

"This is unbelievable," he said.

He turned to his wife and daughter who looked to him an answer.

"Daddy, are we still going to the radio station?" asked Stephanie.

"Don't worry, honey," he responded, "Daddy will make sure you get to the radio station on time."

Mrs. Renner suggested that they take a seat while they tried to decide what to do. Stephanie climbed from her mother to her father and wrapped her arms around his neck. They walked slowly to the nearby seats. They sat silently for a short time before Will Renner spoke.

"Well, Liz, do you have any suggestions on what we should do now?" he asked.

"We can still take a taxi," she responded.

"A taxi from here will probably cost a hundred dollars - maybe more. But, since we have no other choice, I guess we need to do it - that is if there are even any taxis left. Any other suggestions?"

"Just one," she announced as she bent her head to pray.

He sat silently holding his daughter as he watched his wife pray for a miracle. He watched with mixed emotions as she prayed to a God that was taking their daughter away. Numb with pain and exhaustion, he said nothing.

Soon his wife finished and turned back to him.

"We'll find a taxi and will get to the station in plenty of time," she said.

"Okay," he agreed, "I guess that's our only choice."

They stood to gather their belongings when they were approached by a woman who appeared to be in her late forties. She was a fragile looking woman with short brown hair and thick glasses.

"Excuse me," she said to them, "but I couldn't help but overhear your discussion. I understand you need to get to Chicago."

"Yes," responded Mrs. Renner.

"Well," she continued, "I feel a little responsible for your dilemma. You see I just got their last car. So I figure the least I can do is offer you a ride."

"Really," returned Mrs. Renner. "You're going into Chicago?"

"Yes. I'm going home for Christmas - just flew in from Cincinnati. And I would love the company."

Mrs. Renner looked at her husband who just nodded. She turned back to the lady.

"That would be wonderful if it's no trouble. I'm Liz and this is my husband, Will. And this is our daughter Stephanie."

Stephanie opened her eyes and smiled at the lady. "Hi, Mrs. Franklin," she said.

The three looked at each other in confusion.

"I'm sorry, sweetheart," she responded, "but I'm Miss Phillips."

"No," Stephanie insisted, "you're Mrs. Franklin. I knew you would come back for me."

Mrs. Renner turned to the woman. "Mrs. Franklin was Stephanie's Sunday school teacher who recently passed away. You do look a lot like her, although she was about thirty years older."

"I understand," said Miss Phillips to Stephanie. "You can call me Mrs. Franklin if you like, dear."

The four made their way to the rental car. Only a slight dusting of snow covered the area, as a few flurries swirled around in the chilly evening breeze. Mrs. Renner took the front seat next to Miss Phillips, while Will Renner sat in the back seat holding his daughter who had again fallen asleep.

"Now where do you need to go?" she inquired as they left the airport. They explained that they needed to be dropped off at the radio station.

"Oh," she replied slowly, "then you must be the Renners."

"I guess we're quite famous," returned Mr. Renner.

"You know our situation then?" asked Mrs. Renner.

"Yes, from the paper. And I am terribly sorry. I wish there was something I could do."

"You are," returned Mrs. Renner.

They drove mostly in silence, sometimes commenting about the weather or the traffic. They soon discovered that Miss Phillips was going home to spend Christmas with her parents and younger brother who lived only a few miles from the radio station. She soon glanced in the mirror to see Stephanie snuggled in her father's arms.

"Is she all right?" she asked.

"She's pretty weak," he answered. "I wish we had never agreed to make this trip."

"From what I've read about her," she said, "you two didn't have much choice."

"I guess that's true," answered Mrs. Renner with a sad laugh. "She's a pretty strong-willed little girl."

"And one with a lot of faith," added Miss Phillips.

"Yes," said Mr. Renner. "I only wish I had half as much. It's pretty sad when a six-year-old is stronger than her father."

"Oh," said Miss Phillips as she slowly nodded her understanding. "Have you asked God?" she asked.

"Asked Him what?" he asked.

"For strength."

He did not respond but only turned towards the window.

"I can't explain why this is happening, Mr. Renner," she continued, "but sometimes it's better to just try and accept things and ask God for strength to help you through it. Even Jesus called on His Father for strength."

Mr. Renner still did not respond. His silence concerned his wife who turned to him. She saw him with his head bowed against his daughter's brow, his eyes closed.

They arrived at the radio station at eight-forty-five. The snow had intensified as they approached the city, but the roads were still passable. Miss Phillips turned the car into the parking lot next to the radio station. She then got out to help them with their belongings. Stephanie awoke again as they were about to say good-bye.

"Thank you, Mrs. Franklin," she stated as she leaned forward and hugged her neck.

"It's been my pleasure," she said as she gave the child a kiss. "Make sure you tell all the little kids how much Jesus loves them."

"I will," she returned.

Mr. and Mrs. Renner again thanked her for her assistance and said good-bye. She hugged them each, returned to the car and disappeared into the evening.

Mr. Ellis was waiting nervously as they entered the station. He eagerly greeted them.

"I'm glad you made it. I was really worried but didn't know what to do. I heard they'd closed the airport. I forget to get your cell phone number, so I had you paged at Champaign but got no response. I guess you'd already left."

"Yes, a very nice lady gave us a ride," responded Mrs. Renner.

A young Asian woman soon appeared and was introduced as the station manager. Mr. Ellis also pointed out the disc jockey and technician who waved at them through the glass. Stephanie soon awoke again and smiled at Mr. Ellis.

"Hi, Mr. Ellis," she said weakly.

"Hi, honey," he returned as he kissed her forehead. He then pulled Mrs. Renner aside.

"Is she okay," he asked. "She doesn't have to do this if she doesn't have the energy."

"She's pretty weak, but we can't tell her no. We all know what this means to her."

"Okay, you can come with me into the broadcast room to go over a couple of things, and Mr. Renner can sit with Stephanie."

She returned to explain to her husband then left the reception area to enter the broadcast booth. The instructions were very simple. The disc jockey showed her where Stephanie would sit, which microphone to use, and which light would signal her to begin. Once finished with the instructions, Mr. Ellis asked how her husband was doing.

"I really can't say," she returned. "I guess only time will tell."

He nodded his understanding. Mrs. Renner excused herself to use the restroom adjacent to the broadcast booth.

It was a few minutes before nine when she returned from the restroom and walked toward her husband and daughter. She had just started to ask him how their daughter was doing when she looked into his eyes. A tear rolled down his cheek as he gently rubbed his daughter's face. Mrs. Renner stood silently for a moment, her hands covering her mouth, then slowly bent forward and kissed her daughter's forehead. She then seated herself in the chair next to them. They sat silently - all the words had already been spoken.

Mr. Ellis soon returned to the room. Immediately he understood. He knelt in front of them and gently rubbed his fingers through Stephanie's hair.

"I'm sorry," he whispered.

They nodded their heads in understanding. He bent forward and kissed his young friend. As he did so, he noticed a small piece of paper in her hand. He gently removed it and held it up. It was a bookmarker inscribed with a bible verse.

"This must have been very important to her," he stated. He read it aloud. "Jesus said, 'suffer little children, and forbid them not, to come unto me; for such is the Kingdom of Heaven.'"

"Where did she get that?" asked Mrs. Renner. "She didn't have that when we left."

"I would say she just got it from her Sunday school teacher," said her husband.

Mr. Ellis soon arose. "I'll tell the station manager. You two can just wait until I get back."

He turned to leave, but before he reached the door Mr. Renner called to him. "No," he said firmly, "Stephanie had a message to give and I'm going to make sure everyone hears it."

He arose and handed his daughter to his wife, and then walked into the broadcast booth. The disc jockey, who had been observing through the glass, nodded his understanding. They waited in silence for the nine o'clock hour. Soon the red light on the console came on and the disk jockey, without comment, gave him the signal to begin.

"Good evening boys and girls, and ladies and gentlemen," he began. "I am Will Renner. I know you were hoping to hear from our daughter Stephanie tonight, but unfortunately that won't be possible. You see," he continued with a crack in his voice, "just a few minutes ago she went to be with her friend, Jesus."

He stopped for a second and took a deep breath before continuing. "Our daughter, as I'm sure many of you have heard, was quite a remarkable little girl. She has always been a loving, generous child, but even we didn't know how special she was until she became ill. Never once in her illness did she get angry or depressed. And, as you know, her last request was to let other sick children know that they didn't need to be afraid of dying either."

"You see, Stephanie had a special friend in Jesus. She knew that all she had to do was believe in Him and she didn't have to be scared - even of death. She knew that if she died she would be going home to Him. That is the message she wanted to give all the other sick children in the world. That Jesus loves you and if you put your faith in Him you don't have to be afraid of dying."

"Unfortunately for me, maybe because I'm an adult, I didn't have as much faith as Stephanie. I have been very angry and confused about my daughter's illness. I've been trying to understand how a kind and loving God could take such a beautiful little girl away from her parents. I guess this is the question that we all have to ask ourselves sometime in our lives - why do these terrible things happen. And, unfortunately I still don't have the answer to that. But I've been thinking, and praying, about this a lot lately, and I think I've begun to resolve it in my heart."

"Just when I was at my lowest and didn't think I could continue any longer, God sent two special people into my life. I guess some people could say it was just a coincidence, but I don't think so. They helped me understand a lot of things I had been struggling with. And, more importantly, they let me know that, even in all the suffering in this world, God is still good and still hears our prayers."

"I have always said that our daughter was God's greatest gift to us. I was wrong. As much as I love our daughter and always will, what would it matter if she is only with us for a short time and then is taken away? Our greatest gift then is that we can again be together forever in heaven. As the Bible says in John chapter three, verse 16, '*That God so loved the world that He gave His only begotten Son so that whosoever believeth in Him shall not perish but have everlasting life.*'

"The good news, boys and girls, and ladies and gentlemen, is that, although tonight our hearts are full of sadness for our daughter, we will be with her again someday. And tomorrow, Stephanie will be helping her friend, Jesus, celebrate his birthday."

"So, from Stephanie, her mother, and I, I would like to say Merry Christmas to all of you and may God bless you."

Will Renner slowly arose from the seat and returned to the reception area. As he did so the paramedics were taking his daughter and placing her on a stretcher. He and his wife knelt down and gave their daughter a final kiss before they took her away. They watched out the window as they placed her body into the ambulance and drove away.

Mr. Ellis joined them at the window and put his arms around the couple. They watched in silence as the ambulance disappeared into the snow. They then turned their eyes to the sky. In amazement, they watched through the swirling snow as one lone star shone brightly through the night.

THE ROOT OF ALL EVIL

OCTOBER

It was a beautiful, crisp, mid-October day. With the sun's aid, the chilly morning air gradually gave way to a warm and gentle autumn breeze. The fall foliage brought the northern Kentucky countryside alive with color, as a flock of birds drifted overhead on their annual journey south.

It was an unusually warm day in Covington. By afternoon, the temperature reached eighty degrees. With both her husband and son gone for the afternoon, Angela Carey decided it was a good time to complete some outside chores. She began by cleaning the patio furniture. She would, however, let her husband move it to the storage shed when he returned from work. She soon looked up from her work to see a familiar figure approaching.

"Hey, cousin," said her visitor. "Looks like you're hard at work today."

"Hi, Mandy," she returned. "Yeah, I thought I would use this nice weather to finish this. It might be the last warm day we get. What are you doing here?"

"Nothing. Bobby is watching a football game so I just thought I'd stop by. I rang your bell but you didn't answer, so I thought you might be back here. Where's everyone?"

"Donnie's working and Denny is over at one of his friends."

"Donnie's working? On a Saturday?"

"Yeah. A guy came in a few days ago with an old car - a '59 Cadillac, I believe. He just bought it and wanted it painted in time for a show next week in Lexington. Donnie said the car is beautiful. He doesn't even think it needs painting, but the guy is paying them over $3,000 so who are they to argue?"

"Wow, sounds like there should be a nice bonus in it for him."

"That would be nice. I'm sure we could put the money to good use."

Amanda seated herself in a chair that her cousin had just finished cleaning.

"That reminds me of what I wanted to talk to you about, Angela."

"What? Donnie's bonus?" she asked jokingly.

"Well, sort of. I think you and Donnie should go to Barbados with us in January."

"To Barbados?" she responded as she raised an eyebrow. "When did you decide this?"

"Just this morning. We just got back from the travel agent a little while ago. We decided we couldn't take another winter around here without a break. What do you say? Wouldn't you like to go?"

"Of course we would like to, but we can't afford it. How much is this going to cost?"

"It's not that bad - we got a pretty good deal. Including food and everything, it will be around $3,500."

"Wow, that's a lot of money. I appreciate the offer, Mandy, but we just don't have that kind of money. And, if you don't mind me saying so, after what you've been telling me lately, I don't see how you can afford it either."

"We charged it, of course."

"Amanda, I don't see...."

"Angela, don't. I don't want to discuss this again. I know we don't agree on how we handle money, but I just thought it would be nice if you two could join us. Just forget I asked."

"I'm sorry," said Angela as she put down her sponge, "I don't like to preach to you, but I just worry about you two. You're getting deeper and deeper in debt. What if something happens and one of you can't work?"

"There's no such thing as total security in this world, Angie, so why worry. Besides, we only owe about $5,000. That's not even one tenth of our income. That's probably a lot less than some of our friends."

"I'm assuming that $5,000 is not including your trip or your car loans."

"Okay, look," she responded as she got up, "I didn't want to get into this conversation again. I just thought you might like to go with us."

"I'm sorry," replied Angela, "I shouldn't have said anything. And I do appreciate the offer. I'll talk to Donnie and maybe he'll agree. You going to church tomorrow?"

"We're planning on it. If not you can call me."

She was soon gone. Angela walked to the side of the house and watched as her cousin climbed into her new Acura and drove away. For a fleeting second she envied her impulsiveness. Then, as quickly as it had come, the feeling left. She knew her family's direction was the correct one. With a sigh and a shrug of her head, she returned to the patio.

———————

Amanda and Bobby were not in church the following day. Angela was not surprised. They attended infrequently, and she did not expect her to be there after yesterday's conversation. As expected, Donnie agreed with his wife regarding the subject. Although he, too, would have loved a trip to the island, he stated that they would have to save the money first. Perhaps they could afford it the following year.

After church, the Carey family had lunch at a nearby Italian restaurant. At Denny's suggestion, they ordered a large pizza. With his parent's nagging, he also ordered a salad. After the meal, the boy turned to his parents.

"Okay, I have something I want to ask you two."

"What's that, son," asked his father.

"Well, I'm almost seventeen, right?"

"We'll give you that," responded his mother. "Was that the question?"

"Ha, ha. Well, I think it's time I had more freedom."

"Okay," said his father slowly. "Anything in particular or just general?"

"Well, some other guys at school are going on a ski trip during Christmas vacation, and - well, I'd like to go."

"Oh," said his mother. "And where would this ski trip be to?"

"It's...uh...well, to Colorado."

"Nice. And for how long?" she continued.

"Six days."

"That's quite a trip," said his father. "How much do you think something like that might cost?"

"Oh, they're getting a good deal through Johnny Lakein's dad. He's an officer of the ski club."

"How much?" repeated his mother.

"Only $1,100.00."

"And what does that include?" asked his father.

"I knew you'd ask. Everything - airfare, the room, skiing, meals."

"All meals?" asked his mother.

"Well, all breakfasts & four dinners. So what do you say?"

"That does sound like a good deal," said his mother. "Do you actually have $1,100.00?"

"No, not exactly."

"Well, then," said his father, "I'd say this conversation is really about money as well as freedom."

"I guess so," he answered reluctantly. "So what's your answer?"

"Your father and I will talk about it," stated his mother.

"I can't get an answer now?"

"Is it December already?" asked his father.

"Well, I need to know by November 5th."

"I think that gives us enough time to talk," stated his father. "But, seriously, Denny, we know this is important to you, but I just don't know if we can afford it. We'll talk about it and let you know this week."

They continued to discuss the details of the trip. It was clear from their son's expression that he was unhappy about their response - or lack of one.

"Was there something else you wanted to say?" asked his mother.

"Well, yeah," he returned. "Since you asked, there's something I just don't understand. You give a hundred dollars to the church every week, but every time I ask for money you say you don't have it or you have to think about it. I think you care more for the church than you do for me."

Angela and Donnie looked at each other in surprise. His father turned back to his son and said, "Well, son, we're glad that you would share that with us. But let's look at what you said. First, do you feel like there's ever been a time when your basic needs have not been met?"

"Yeah, like when..."

"No, I'm not talking about wants or desires. I'm talking about the basics that every parent owes his children - food, clothing, shelter, an education, medical care, Pizza."

"No," he responded as he tried to suppress a laugh at his last comment.

"So, I guess it's really your wants and desires which you feel haven't been met?"

"Well, if you put it that way. I mean, I know I'm not starving and I have clothes and a place to live. But you make it sound like nothing else is important."

"We're not saying they're not important," added his mother, "but it's important to keep things in perspective. And I don't think your father and I ask any more from you than we do ourselves."

"Well, you sure spend a lot more frivolously than I do."

"Really?" asked his father. "Can you give us a couple of examples?"

"Like on your cars, the house, stuff for work."

"And those things are frivolous?" laughed his mother. "Look son, your father drives an eight year-old car. I drive a newer car because your dad doesn't want you and I to break down somewhere on a deserted road. And the money we spend on the house is for all of us."

Denny thought for a minute. The approach he had taken had not gained the desired results. He thought he might have better results with a different issue.

"Well, what about your savings, then?" he asked.

"What about our savings?" asked his father.

"You're always putting money in savings and investments but then we can never afford to do anything. And, like Mandy says, who knows what might happen tomorrow?"

His father gave a quick shake of his head, then turned to his wife and asked, "Do you have your bible with you?"

She reached into her purse and removed her bible and handed it to her husband.

"Great," said Denny. "You always carry that with you?"

"Not always…just when you're around."

"Rather than argue with us," said his father, "why don't we see what God has to say about these things."

"Dad…," he began to object, but then stopped when he saw the look in his father's eyes.

"First, let's look at your question about saving. Let's try Proverbs, Chapter six, verse six. He began to read.

"Go to the ant, thou sluggard; consider her ways, and be wise:"

He stopped and turned to his son.

"Do you know what a sluggard is?"

"Yes, it's a snail."

"Well," laughed his father, "that's close. It's a lazy person." He continued to read.

"Which having no guide, overseer, or ruler, provideth her meat in the summer, and gathereth her food in the harvest. How long wilt thou sleep, O sluggard? When wilt thou rise out of thy sleep: Yet a little sleep, a little slumber, a little folding of the hands to sleep: So shall thy poverty come as one that travelleth, and thy want as an armed man."

He turned back to his son.

"I bet you didn't know that story was from the bible, did you?"

"No," he returned quickly, "and what's amazing is that my friends and I were just wondering the other day where the ant story came from."

His parents laughed before his father continued.

"So, do you understand what God's saying?" asked his father.

"Yeah. It says don't be lazy and store up your food while you can."

"Yeah, basically. Or build up your savings while you can. And did you get the part at the end that says that if you don't you will end up in poverty waiting to rob someone."

"I got it, Dad," he answered. "Will this lesson be over soon?"

"Soon enough," continued his father, "let's look at what it says about budgeting & spending. Let's first look at Second Peter, chapter two, verse 19. He read: "For by what a man is overcome, by this he is enslaved.""

He waited for a response but got none.

"Let's also look at one other verse," he continued as he searched the Bible's concordance. "How about Proverbs, chapter 13, verse 18." He read: "Poverty and shame shall come to him who neglects discipline."

He again turned to his son, whom he knew by now was wishing

he had never begun the conversation.

"What does that mean to you?"

"I don't know, Dad," he returned. "I guess that you have to have self-discipline."

"Exactly. And what if you don't?"

"I don't know. That's not talking about money anyway."

"Not just money, I guess, but what fits better here? More people are overcome and enslaved by money than any other thing."

"Okay, Dad. I get the picture."

"There's still one more issue you brought up," said his mother. "And we wouldn't want any of your concerns to go unanswered, son."

He looked at her, not certain if her remark was meant to be sarcastic. He felt it best to let it pass.

"Okay, let's see what God says about giving to the church," said his father. "Let's look at First John, chapter three, verse seventeen." He read: "But whoso hath this world's good, and seeth his brother hath need, and shutteth up his bowels of compassion from him, how dwelleth the love of God in him?"

"Let's look at one other area," he continued.

"Proverbs chapter three, verse nine says, `Honour the Lord with thy substance, and with the firstfruits of all thine increase.'"

"So what do those verses mean to you, Dad?" asked Denny, before his father could speak.

"Well, son," he answered with a laugh, "I guess it means we've been instructed to give a portion of everything to the church. And, if we don't, how can we say that we have the love of God in us. What do you think?"

"I think you're right," returned Denny, in a tone that let them know he wished the conversation to be over.

Angela listened intently to their con-versation, hoping that their son really understood what they were saying. She knew, with a teenager, it would not be a long wait to see if the message had gotten through.

One of the things that Angela liked most about her job in the school cafeteria was that she could, to a small degree, monitor her son's activities. The thing that her son hated most about his mother's job in the school cafeteria was that she could, to any degree, monitor his activities. Even so, it was a situation to which he had learned to adjust. As patiently as possible for any teenager, he waited in her car after school. She had hardly gotten the door closed when he turned to her.

"So, Mom, have you and Dad talked about the ski trip yet?"

"Jees, Denny," she responded, "it's only been one day. We told you we'd talk this week."

"Okay," he responded, "I just thought I'd ask."

"I'm sorry, son," she said as she turned to him. I'll talk to him tonight. But I don't want you to get your hopes up."

"Okay. I know you'll do what's best," he said with a coy smile.

Angela patted her son on the leg and smiled. She knew how lucky they were to have such a good kid. She believed that the morals they had tried to instill in him had helped shape his personality. But she also knew that there were no guarantees on how a child would turn out. The best they could do was to be the kind of parents that God intended them to be and leave the rest to Him.

She also knew how difficult it was to be a teenager - especially in these senseless times. She understood the challenges and temptations the kids had to face each day. She also understood the impact peer pressure could have on a young boy or girl. For that reason, she was concerned about their answer regarding his ski trip. Still, she knew they had to do what was right and hope their son was mature enough to accept their answer.

As usual, Donnie returned home promptly at six-fifteen. He kissed his wife, rubbed his son's hair, and washed his hands at the kitchen sink. Although she was certain their son did not notice, she knew her husband was upset about something. She felt it better to wait until they were alone before discussing it.

Angela waited until the dinner dishes had been cleared and Denny had left the room before turning to her husband. "So do you want to tell me what's wrong?" she asked as her husband poured himself a cup of coffee.

"And I thought I was doing so well," he returned with a smile. "What gave me away?"

"About seventeen years of marriage. Do you want to discuss it?"

"Sure. I just wanted to talk to you alone first. The transmission began acting up on my Oldsmobile today, so I had a mechanic look at it. It looks like it'll cost almost two grand to replace."

"Wow, I had no idea transmissions cost so much. Where's the car?" she asked as she looked out the window.

"It's still at work. That's Enrico's pickup. He said he won't need it for a while."

"That's good. You're lucky to work for such a decent guy. But can't you contact one of the garages you work with to get the work done cheaper?"

"We did. That is cheaper. It just happens that that transmission is one of the most expensive Oldsmobile ever made. They said it may be less but they wanted to give me the worse case scenario."

"Oh, well," she said with a shrug of her shoulders, "there's nothing we can do. We've got almost four thousand in savings. We're lucky we have the money."

"That's true," responded Donnie, "but it's not the car that's worrying me. Angela, with this happening I don't see any way we will have the money to let Denny go on that trip."

"Oh, that's right," she returned. "I almost forgot about that. He's going to be very upset. You don't think there's anyway we can swing it?"

"Well, it could be two thousand for this, and we have Christmas coming up. If we pay for his trip we will have zilch in our savings. I just don't see any way. I know he'll be upset but it will be a good lesson for him. He'll have greater disappointments in his life. It's time he learns how to deal with them now."

"But we have some money in an IRA. Maybe we could take some from there."

"And with taxes and penalties a thousand dollars will cost us fifteen hundred or more. No, I think we just have to tell him that he'll have to wait until next year."

She knew he was right. And she agreed that it would be a good lesson for him. It was just very difficult to deny her son something he wanted so badly.

"Well," she said slowly, "I guess we might as well tell him."

Donnie went to his son's room and told him they would like to talk to him. They seated themselves in the living room, he and his wife on the couch and their son in a nearby chair. Donnie explained the situation with his car. Before he could saying anything more his son interrupted.

"So, I guess this means that once more Denny gets screwed!"

"Denny!" said his mother harshly, "you will not speak to us like that. Do you think your father planned for the transmission to go out so you wouldn't be able to go on your trip?"

"Look, son," said his father more calmly, "I know how important this is to you and I'm sorry that we have to tell you no, but I think you should be mature enough to understand when something like this happens. This is reality. Things like this will happen to you the rest of your life and you have to learn to adjust to them."

"I just know that if this happened to one of my friend's family, they would still be able to go."

"Well, son," said his mother irritably, "we're sorry we're not as rich as some of your friends. I guess when you get older you can become rich and have everything you want. Right now you're stuck with us."

"Are we through yet?"

Donnie looked at his wife, then back to his son. Perhaps there was another solution.

"Maybe there's another way for you to go on this trip, son."

"What do you mean?" he asked.

"My boss has been thinking about hiring someone part-time to help around the shop, and you're old enough to start working. If you're interested, I could talk to him. You could probably make fifty to seventy-five a week. With what you have in your bank now, by the time the trip rolls around you would have enough saved to go. I think it's about time you started becoming responsible for your own finances anyway."

"There's only one problem with that, Dad," his son stated. "I have to have the deposit next week and the rest of it has to be paid by December 1st."

"How much is the deposit?"

"A hundred dollars."

"Well, we'll pay the deposit, but you'll have to pay us back."

Denny looked at his parent's for a moment, then arose from the chair.

"No thanks," he stated dryly as he headed for his room, "I'll just stay home."

His mother opened her mouth to call after him but his father raised his hand to quiet her. They watched as their son walked angrily to his room. They both knew that his refusal to go was his way of punishing them. Donnie wondered if they had made the right decision. He wanted to teach his son responsibility, but was this the proper way to do it? Suddenly the bible verse, Second Thessalonians, chapter 3, verse 30 flashed into his mind: "For even when we were with you, this we commanded you, that if any would not work, neither should he eat." He knew they had made the right decision.

DECEMBER

It was the first week of December and the Cincinnati area had received its first substantial snowfall of the year. Over three inches of snow covered the rolling Ohio and Kentucky hills. Much to the children's dismay, however, the snow had not been disruptive enough to close the school - only delay their opening a couple of hours.

Angela Carey and her son arrived home from school at three-thirty. Since it was her cousin Amanda's day off, Angela had made plans to deliver unused Christmas decorations to her house. With her son's help, she soon had the decorations loaded into her car.

She thanked him for his help, kissed him good-bye, and left for her cousin's house. There had been little discussion regarding the ski trip since their conversation in October. Angela had hoped that Denny would have come to them and apologized for his attitude, but he had not. Nor had he agreed to accept the job as his father had recommended. But, neither had he complained about the situation again. Angela hoped that he had begun to understand their decision. Only time would tell if that was the case.

With her hands full of decorations, Angela pressed her elbow to the doorbell at her cousin's house. It was a newer home in a middle class neighborhood. Amanda had told her that they had paid $250,000 for the home - not extravagant by current standards, but still a heavy burden for a family making under $60,000 a year. The mortgage payment itself was not the problem - it was the two car payments and the fine furniture that made Angela wonder how they even managed to eat. Of course, it was none of her business - a fact that she needed to remind herself before entering.

Her cousin opened the door and invited her inside, then helped her place the decorations on the dining room table. Mandy thanked her for her generosity and invited her into the kitchen for a cup of tea. Angela accepted, saying that she could only stay for a short time. The two chatted about the upcoming holidays. They discussed which of their mothers, who were sisters, would host this year's Christmas dinner. Each year the procedure was the same - their mothers would debate the issue until the week before Christmas, at which time their husbands would demand a decision be made. Angela truly believed that her mother and aunt enjoyed the ritual more than Christmas dinner itself.

Amanda soon turned to her cousin with a more serious look. "Well, Angie," she began, "this hasn't been a good week. It seems like you are psychic or something. I just lost my job."

"Wow," she responded. "I'm so sorry to hear that. When did that happen?"

"Just a few days ago. I didn't feel like going into it over the phone."

"I'm really sorry, Mandy. How did it happen? I would have thought, with the increase in construction in the past couple of years, your company would be doing great."

For the past four years, Amanda had worked as a secretary in a small manufacturing firm. The company made electrical fixtures which it sold mostly to new home builders.

"Well, competition has been really rough this past year. A couple of large nationwide companies have won contracts from us, so the president announced some cost-cutting measures. The first was to let go everyone with less than five years service."

"That's terrible. What are you going to do?"

"Well, starting next week, I'll go out and look for another job. Hopefully, it won't take too long."

"I'll have to say," continued Angela, "you're certainly taking it a lot better than I would. I wouldn't have even known something was wrong if you hadn't told me."

"Oh, I'm upset, but what can I do? Like I said before, there's no security in this world."

Angela thought for a moment before asking her next question. She knew she ran the risk of upsetting her again, but she felt it would be worth it if she could help her through this difficult time.

"What are you going to do about your trip? Are you two still going?"

"Well, we've already paid for it."

"But can't you get most of your money back? It's still over a month."

"Actually, as of yesterday, it's less than a month. That means we would forfeit one half of our money, so we've decided to just go ahead and go."

"You don't think it would be worthwhile to cancel and save almost $2,000?"

"Look, Angie, I know you're trying to help, but we'll be fine. Bobby is still working and he makes a lot more than I do. And I know I'll find a job within a few weeks. But I'll agree with one thing you've always said. Money is the root of all evil."

"Actually, the verse says that the love of money is the root of all kinds of evil. And that's because what you love shows where your heart is and what's important to you."

"Thank you for that editorial comment," returned Amanda. "I didn't know I was so materialistic."

"Oh, I'm sorry," said Angela. "I didn't mean that the way it sounded, but it's an area where we all have a problem. We have to be careful about our attitude towards money because it affects such a huge part of our life."

"I know," returned Amanda more calmly. "And I know I'm just a little sensitive right now. I appreciate your advice, Angie, but we'll be fine. Really."

"Okay," she returned, "just let us know if there's something we can do."

Angela gave her cousin a hug before leaving. As she left she wondered if there was something more she should have said or done. She soon realized that there was only one other thing to do. After entering her car she dropped her head and prayed.

Angela's mother won the battle to host Christmas dinner. Donnie asked, as he did every year, why her mother and sister could not simply alternate hosting Christmas dinner. And Angela told him, as she did every year, that that would be too simple. However, with rare exception, that was how it turned out.

Dinner began shortly after five o'clock. There were over twenty family members crowded around the dining room and other makeshift tables. Angela's brother was there with his wife and two children, as was Amanda's older, unmarried sister, who had just flown in from Cleveland. Angela never felt close to Jennifer. Perhaps it was because she was five years older than her, or perhaps it was because they just seemed to have nothing in common. Jennifer had put her career above everything else, a philosophy of life so different from hers. Regardless, they were always polite and civil towards each other.

As always, the dinner was wonderful. The holiday music could hardly be heard above the chatter. With so many people present, Angela had little chance to talk to Amanda. She did know, however, that she had not yet found another job. She also surmised that the situation was beginning to bother Amanda much more than she wished to admit. She noticed that she was more somber than normal, and that she had hardly eaten her dinner. She wished to talk to her - to see what assistance she may provide, but decided against it. For once, she would wait until her help was requested.

After dinner, the crowd began to disperse to different parts of the house. Those designated to clean the table and wash the dishes began to do so. Angela volunteered herself, and, much to his dismay, her son. Donnie strolled into the back yard to watch the children playing with their new Christmas toys. He was soon joined by Amanda's husband, Bobby. They watched the children playing, talking casually. Donnie felt a tension coming from Bobby. He chose, however, to say nothing. Soon Bobby turned to him.

"Donnie," he began, "can I ask you for a favor?"

"Sure. What's that?"

"Well, you know about Mandy being out of work."

"Yeah, that's a bummer. Especially this time of year."

"Yeah, well, unfortunately it's getting worse."

"She still can't find anything, huh?"

"No, but that's not what I mean. Mandy's going to have to have surgery."

"Wow," exclaimed Donnie. "Is it serious?"

"No, not really," he answered. "She's going to have to have her gallbladder removed. It's a pretty routine operation - nothing to worry about. And it's not an emergency but the doctor wants it done in the next couple of weeks - -before another flare-up."

"Boy, when it rains, it pours."

"Yeah, and we each had our own insurance, and since she lost her job she's not covered. I can add her to mine, but it's not going to cover this situation."

"I'm sorry to hear that, Bobby. How can we help?"

"Well, as you can imagine, money was tight enough as it was. Now, with this it's obviously going to be worse."

"So, you need to borrow some money?"

"Oh, no," he returned quickly. "That's not what I'm asking, but I could use your help."

"How's that?"

"Well, I'm going to have to sell my car, and I'll be needing some very basic transportation. Do you think your boss might have something reliable he can sell cheap? He gets cars like that sometimes doesn't he?"

"Yeah, sure. I'll ask him. You're selling your Corvette?"

"Yeah, it's only a few years old so it should be worth over thirty grand. We didn't put down a lot on it, but I still should have about ten thousand equity in it. I figure if I can find something dependable for under three grand we will still have almost enough to cover the operation. The rest we'll have to put on our charge cards."

"Well, I'm sorry you're going to have to sell your car, but yeah, sure, I'll ask Enrico if he has anything. I guess this means your vacation is cancelled, too?"

"Yeah, unfortunately. I guess it could of been worse. We could have had to cancel the last day and had to pay the entire amount instead of only half."

"That's still a lot of money though."

"Yeah, almost two thousand dollars."

"You sure there's nothing else we can do?"

"No, but I appreciate your asking. We'll be fine."

The two continued talking for a few minutes before returning to the house. Donnie was sorry to hear about their problems. At least Amanda's problem was not serious, and from what he knew, the operation would be a fairly simple one. He hoped, but did not expect, that these problems would help them learn to handle their finances.

The table was soon cleared, allowing Denny to return to the living room. He seated himself next to Amanda. The two were soon joking and laughing together. Angela was glad that her son had such a good relationship with her cousin. Unfortunately, she knew that much of his admiration for her was for her carefree lifestyle. As impressionable as he was, she could only pray that he would not pick up her philosophy towards money. She felt that her concerns were justified. Even though Denny had not mentioned it, she knew he was still upset over their refusal to pay for his ski trip. He had, however, on various occasions, mentioned Amanda and Bobby's trip to the Caribbean. Angela knew it was his way of making her feel guilty - a tactic which, she unfortunately had to admit, worked. But, guilt or not, she knew they had made the right decision. Hopefully in time her son would realize it also.

Upon his return to work, Donnie spoke to his boss, Enrico, about a car for Bobby. Enrico, having met Bobby and Amanda on several occasions, was curious as to why they would need another, and older, car. Donnie explained the situation to him. For a reason unknown to Donnie, Enrico seemed more than a little curious about their financial problems. Since he was asking him for his help, however, Donnie felt an obligation to discuss the situation. The conversation did, however, give Donnie an opportunity to present his beliefs on how one should manage their finances. He was just a little surprised that Enrico seemed to take such an interest in the subject.

Somewhat to his surprise, Enrico informed him that he did have a car available.

"It's the 92 Toyota Camry that we just finished painting. The guy just called me Christmas Eve and told me he's not going to have the money to pay me so he's just going to give me the car. He's coming in this afternoon to sign over the title."

"You're kidding," said Donnie. "What kind of shape is it in?"

"Well, it has well over a hundred thousand miles, but it seems to be in good mechanical condition. At least it has a nice new paint job."

"How much do you want for it?"

"Just what we have in it - about fourteen hundred."

Donnie called Bobby to inform him of the car. He said he would like the car and asked if Enrico could hold it until he sold his. He agreed to hold it for a week.

Bobby called Donnie the following Sunday afternoon to inform him that he had sold his car. They made arrangements to pick up the Toyota the following Tuesday.

JANUARY

Amanda stared out the window at the snow-covered landscape. From her bed she could see the children riding their sleds down the hill behind her house. The overnight snowfall had given them an unexpected day's vacation. Unfortunately, she could not share in their joy. The snow only reminded her of the sandy beach at Barbados where she and her husband were to have been this week. Instead, she lie in bed recovering from her operation. Even though it had been a week since the surgery, she was still quite sore. She felt that, within the past few weeks, her whole life had fallen apart. First she had lost her job, then she had discovered she needed surgery. And, since her insurance had expired with her job, her husband had been forced to sell his car to pay for the operation. And now she realized it would be at least another two to three weeks before she could even begin looking for another job.

She forced herself out of bed, threw on her robe, and cautiously descended the stairs. Angela would be by soon to check on her. She put the coffee on and poured herself a bowl of cereal. She had begun pouring the coffee when the doorbell rang. She slowly made herself to the door and greeted her cousin.

"Well," said Angela, "you're looking better."

"You're kidding," she answered. "I look half-dead."

"Like I said," joked Angela, "you're looking a little better."

The two walked slowly into the kitchen. Amanda seated herself at the table as Angela finished pouring the coffee and brought it to her.

"Can I get you anything else?" asked Angela

"Yeah. A new life."

"You've had it bad for a while."

"Yeah. I wonder what will happen next."

The two continued to talk about her surgery and recovery. Angela provided no more unsolicited advice regarding their financial situation. Soon, however, Amanda made an unexpected statement.

"Well, Angie," she began, "Bobby and I have made a decision on how to get ourselves out of this mess."

"Oh, what is that?"

"We're going to rent out our house and move back in with my parents for a year."

"Really? Why did you decide to do that?"

"Well it should be no surprise. You know our situation. Bobby didn't get as much as he wanted for the car, and the operation cost even more than we expected, so we had to withdraw what little we had in savings and put the rest on the charge card. I don't know when

I'll find a job. We can rent this place out for about eight hundred a month, and my parents will let us live there for free. It should only take about a year before we get all our bills paid off."

"Wow," responded Angela, "I'm sorry to hear that, Mandy. I know that was a difficult decision to make. Is there anything I can do?"

"Just one thing."

"What's that?"

"Don't say 'I told you so'."

"Mandy," she returned, "I'm sorry if I've given you the wrong impression. The advice I gave was never to prove that I was right or smarter than you. It's only because I love you and worry about you."

"Oh, I know that, Angie," she said more calmly. "I know you're only concerned about what's best for us, but we have to make our own decisions. Besides, even if I had listened to everything you had ever said, there's no reason to believe that this wouldn't have happened."

"I'm not sure I agree with that."

"So are you saying that because you have a different attitude towards money that something like this couldn't happen to you? What if Donnie lost his job or if you or Denny had a major illness? You could end up in the same condition we're in."

"Well, I guess that's true. There's no total security on this planet. The only real security is in knowing and trusting God."

"Oh, I know that, Angela," she returned. "We're both Christians, but that's not what I'm talking about now. I'm talking about security in this world. And I don't believe that your way of doing things provides any more security than ours."

"Well, I'm sorry, but I disagree. There are many Bible verses that instruct us to budget our money and save for difficult times. Even though we can't foresee every problem or emergency, I think we have a responsibility to plan for the unseen - even if for no other reason than so we won't be a burden to our families and society. But I don't think that's really what this is about."

"What do you mean?"

"Well, I can think of two Bible verses; the one you mentioned before, First Timothy chapter six, verse ten. 'For the love of money is a root of all kinds of evil: which some reaching after have been led astray from the faith, and have pierced themselves through with many sorrows.' And Matthew chapter nineteen, verse 24: 'It is easier for a camel to go through the eye of a needle than for a rich man to enter the kingdom of God.'"

"I don't follow you," stated Amanda. "What are you saying?"

"Well, it's like I said before - and I'm not talking about just you or Bobby - it applies to everyone. I think our attitude towards money - perhaps more than any other thing - reflects our relationship with God. If we're not careful we can end up worshiping money - which I think most people in our society do. And the more money we make, the more prideful we become. We forget that even our ability to be successful comes from God. We end up thinking we are so self-sufficient that we don't need God."

She stopped and looked at Amanda, waiting for a comment. Receiving none, she continued.

"Well?"

"Well, what?" returned Amanda.

"Am I preaching to you again?"

"Probably, but it's okay. Go on."

"Well, I guess that's about it. I can only think of one other thing."

"What's that?"

"The only thing that God asks in return for all the riches He has given us - and that is for us to return a small portion of everything we make to Him. And, if we don't budget our money we can't even do that."

She again waited for a reply but received none.

"Well, that's all I have to say. What do you think?"

"I think," said Amanda pensively, "that you've given me a lot to think about. And I will think about it. I still think, however, that we will have to go ahead with the plans we have made to get back on track."

"I guess you're right. There's only one thing I would like to ask."

"What's that?"

"Before you do anything, pray about it."

"I guess that's another weakness for us. Bobby and I will have to talk about it."

Angela visited for a few minutes longer before arising to leave. As she did so, she reached forward and gave Amanda a hug.

"I'll call you later to see if you need anything."

She then turned and left her house. As she drove away, she looked back to see Amanda waving from the window.

———————

Donnie entered the body shop where he worked and had begun removing his coat when his boss greeted him. Enrico informed him he would like to talk to him in his office when he had a chance. Donnie removed his boots, poured himself a cup of coffee, and walked into his boss's office.

Enrico was the owner, as well as the manager, of the body shop. Donnie enjoyed working for him. He was an honest and fair man. Donnie, whenever given the opportunity, had shared his Christian beliefs with Enrico, although he was still uncertain of his beliefs. Enrico was a very private person. It was rare that he spoke of his personal life, and even rarer that he discussed the management of the business with his employees.

Donnie entered his boss's office and seated himself near his desk. Enrico closed his appointment book and pushed it aside.

"So what's going on, boss? Is everything okay?"

"Oh, sure, Donnie. No problem. I just wanted to thank you for your help."

"For my help? Sure - any time. But, uh, exactly what help would that be?"

Enrico smiled and pushed his chair back from the desk. "Do you remember a few weeks ago when you asked if I had a car for your cousin?"

"Sure," he answered, "and I really appreciate your help."

"No problem. Well, if you remember, we spent some time talking about what the Bible says about handling money."

"Yeah, I remember."

"Well, I know you were directing that toward your cousin and her husband, but I felt as if you were talking directly to me."

"Oh, I'm sorry, Enrico. I didn't intend it to sound that way."

"Oh, no, Donnie, that's quite okay. As a matter of fact, it was just what I needed."

"What do you mean?"

"Well, as you know, I don't usually discuss business or personal matters with my employees but...well, I think you have a right to know this. I'd been thinking of buying a second location."

"Really?"

"Yes. It's a little shop on the other side of town. It hasn't been managed very well so the owner was pretty eager to sell. I could have gotten a good price on it, so I felt it would be a good long-term investment but, because of all their problems I would have had to take on a lot of debt. I really was at a loss for what to do. Then, after our conversation, I at least knew where to look."

"Really?"

"Yeah. Believe it or not, I had a strong Christian upbringing. I had just strayed away for a while. Anyway, that night I went home and searched the Bible for anything I could on managing money. I soon found what I needed - Proverbs 22, verse seven."

"The rich ruleth over the poor, and the borrower is the servant to the lender," said Donnie.

"Exactly. That helped me make the decision. I told them I couldn't do it."

"Well, great," stated Donnie. "I mean, if you are still sure you made the right decision."

"Oh yes. As a matter of fact I have since found out that the business is in worse shape than I thought. I made the right decision. So I just wanted to thank you for your help."

"Hey, boss, it wasn't me. I just repeated what it says in the Bible."

"I know, but I appreciate your leading me in the right direction anyway."

Enrico reached forward and grasped Donnie's hand. He smiled and left his office, eager to begin his workday.

FEBRUARY

Amanda called Angela to inform her that they had found a tenant for their house and that they would, as planned, be moving in with her parents. She asked if she and Donnie could help them move the following Saturday.

"Denny and I will be there," she answered, "but Donnie has to work Saturday morning. He can join us in the afternoon, though."

"Sounds great. Thanks."

The moving van was in front of Amanda and Bobby's house as Angela and Denny turned the corner. Angela glanced in her son's direction as they grew nearer. He had a pensive, but sad, look in his eyes.

Angela parked the car across the street and shut off the engine. Instead of opening the door, however, her son sat silently, staring at the house.

"Is something wrong?" she asked.

"No, not really. I was just thinking about something," he returned.

"What's that?"

"Well, Mom, do you think that I would still be able to get a job at Dad's garage?"

"I don't know. What's changed your mind?"

"Well, let's just say that I don't want anyone calling me a sluggard."

She smiled as she rubbed her fingers through her son's hair. The two left the car and walked across the street to their cousin's house.

BEHEMOTH

Much to Cecilia Montero's dismay, though not her surprise, the state of Maryland was again working on the roads. Although it was a necessity, especially after the potholes left over from the many winter storms, she wished there were some way to accomplish it without the horrendous traffic jams. She was, however, luckier - or perhaps smarter - than most. She tried to ignore the pain in her abdomen as she turned her Honda Accord down a side street and weaved her way through the residential neighborhood. She was soon at her destination - American University, in Northwest Washington D.C. After pulling her car into the space bearing her name, she removed her briefcase and walked hurriedly to her class.

She entered the classroom with five minutes to spare. The room was alive with chatter as the students began to take their seats. There were more than a hundred students in her Freshman Ancient History class. As classes go, this one was better than most. The majority of the students were attentive, and the few who weren't were easily controlled by a quick stare. And it appeared that most everyone in the class had at least a small interest in history. After the class had settled, she walked to the front of the room, leaned against her desk, and said, "If you will remember from Friday, we left off at the first century, A.D. The Romans had invaded and captured

England. They then began their march north into Scotland. Well, I think there's an interesting bit of history here. The Romans sent a legion of soldiers into the Highlands and encountered a ferocious and warlike people. Now, I'm sure that the Roman army could have defeated the Highlanders in a battle, but they decided it wasn't worth the effort. They decided there was nothing there that they really needed. And they also felt that the natives were so primitive and barbaric that they were not even worth trying to civilize - they were a couple of rungs down on the evolutionary ladder. So what did the Romans do? To keep them in their place they built a stone wall across northern England. It was about twenty feet high and six to eight feet wide. They stationed sentries all along the wall with a garrison of soldiers nearby. It was named Hadrian's wall, after the Roman Emperor in charge at the time. The wall stood until the Romans withdrew, at which time the Highlanders came down from the mountains and took the wall apart to build houses."

Professor Montero was glad to see that the class enjoyed the story. It led to a great deal of discussion. She preferred the interactive style of teaching. Besides making it easy on her, she knew the students learned much more when they participated rather than when they just listened. Before she knew it the class was over.

She remained at her desk after the class to answer questions or discuss any relevant issues. The room had almost emptied as she gathered her belongings. When she looked up, she saw one remaining student nearing her desk. He seemed shy, almost reticent about approaching her. With a hundred students it was impossible to become familiar with more than a few. She did, however, attempt to at least remember the names of those she met. She had spoken to Brian Haggerty on a couple of other occasions. He was a good, if somewhat serious, student.

"Mr. Haggerty," she asked, "what can I do for you?"

"Professor Montero," he replied in a meek voice, "may I talk to you about something?"

"That's why I'm here. Please sit down."

She directed him toward the lone chair near her desk and waited for him to begin. He seemed to be having difficulty gathering his thoughts.

"Is there something wrong?" she asked.

"Well," he stated, "not exactly wrong. It's just that... I hope you will understand this but...well there's something bothering me about what you said today. Actually it's not the first time you've made reference to it and...well, I just wanted to tell you how I feel."

"Go ahead. I'm listening."

"You stated that the Highlanders were a couple of rungs down on the evolutionary ladder."

"Yes."

"Well, I know it sounds trivial, but that's just like stating that evolution is a fact, when in reality it's just a theory."

"Oh," she nodded, "and I take it you don't believe in evolution?"

"No, I don't."

"Well, Mr. Haggerty," she continued, "you don't have to worry about sharing your beliefs with me. I don't take that as a reflection on my teaching. However, I have to tell you that I disagree with you, and I have to teach what I believe."

"That's fine, but I'm not sure that I see what it has to do with Ancient History."

"I'm afraid I can't agree there either. Where else would it be better suited? I mean, history goes all the way back to the beginning of time, right?"

"I guess," he conceded, "but if you're going to discuss the origins of man, I think you should also consider the possibility that man was created rather than evolved."

She thought for a moment before answering. Since he seemed so young and impressionable, she wanted to make sure that she treated his opinions with respect - as wrong as they might be.

"So, you obviously believe that mankind was created by God just as it is recorded in the Bible?"

"Yes, ma'am."

"Well, then what about all the fossils that prove that evolution occurred?"

"Well, Professor Montero," he stated relaxing somewhat, "I'm not an expert in the subject, but I have read a little about it. As far as I know there have never been any fossils that prove evolution. A hundred years ago the evolutionists used fossils as an example to prove their case. Now, most of them admit that they have to prove evolution in spite of what the fossils show."

"In spite of the fossils?"

"Yes. If evolution were true, Why are there are no transitional fossils?"

"There are plenty of transitional fossils."

"I think all of the fossils show animals adapting among the species, not evolving into a new species. As far as I know, there are no fossils of a half-fish, half-bird."

"I think you're wrong, but right now I can't give you an example. I'll have to get back to you on that."

"And why are there no fossils of man evolving from an ape?"

"There are many fossils of early man - Peking Man, Java Man to name a couple."

"That's true, there are a few fossils which some anthropologists call early man, but they base their findings on the shape of a man's head and the size of his brain. There are really two distinct differences between a man and an ape. A man has five toes in front while an ape has four in front and one in back, and an ape has a tail while a man doesn't. If we evolved from an ape, why are there no fossils showing the toe moving to the front or the tail shrinking? And if it were true, then why didn't all the apes evolve into man? And if it were because different species evolve at different rates, why there are no half-man, half-ape today?"

"You said you didn't know much about this. Sounds to me as though you know quite a bit."

"Well," he answered with a slight smile, "I guess I have studied it a bit."

"Mr. Haggerty, since it appears you know so much about the subject, I have a question for you."

"Yes?"

"Do you take the Bible literally?"

"Generally - yes, I do."

"How can you say generally?"

"Because there are places where it's meant to be taken literally, and other places where it isn't."

"Give me examples."

"Well, such as when Jesus said that we should pluck out our eye rather than look on something sinful. I don't think He meant that we should really blind ourselves, but He was just showing how important it is to control what we look upon."

"I guess I can agree with that, but what about Noah's Ark? Do you take it literally?"

"Yes."

"Mr. Haggerty, I don't want to insult your beliefs, but that's a totally incredulous story. Two of every creature on one boat? You'll have to admit, that's pretty unbelievable."

"Do you know how big the Ark was?"

"Longer than a football field."

"Yes," he laughed. "I'm sure Noah would like that analogy. It was actually almost 500 feet long - almost two football fields - 75 feet wide, and 50 feet high."

"I know that's a big boat, but Mr. Haggerty, two of every living creature?"

"Yes, but there are a couple of other things which you may not be aware."

"Somehow I expected that. Like what?"

"First, the animals were very young - just old enough to be weaned from their mothers. That would mean they were all much smaller than adults."

"Even if that were true there would still be tens of thousands of animals. That's impossible."

"That brings me to my next point. It wasn't necessary to bring aboard every animal - just representatives from each Genus. A pair of dogs would represent the entire canine family, a pair of cats for the feline family, and so on. Each of them had the genetic blueprint for the whole species. That's why the Bible said, 'each animal after its kind.'"

"Hum," she said as she considered his words. "That's really interesting, Mr. Haggerty. But to me it seems like that proves the theory of evolution."

"How's that?"

"If there were only two dogs to represent the entire canine kingdom, and there are dozens of breeds today, how else did they get here?"

"That's really not evolution - that's adaptation. We know today that subspecies can mate with each other. I mean, one breed of dog can mate with another breed just as one breed of cat can mate with another. As far as I know, there has never been a documented case of one species evolving into another life form, or one species, like a cat, mating with another species, like a dog."

"I see," she returned. "One other question then. How did all of these animals get to the Ark? You would have to have animals from every part of the globe. And why would they come? They just decided to show up one day?"

"Professor Montero," answered Mr. Haggerty, "If God can create the universe He can certainly direct animals to do what He wants. And as far as them coming from different parts of the globe, isn't it common knowledge that at one time all continents were connected? It wasn't until after the flood that the continents began to drift apart."

Professor Montero sat pondering his words. It was obvious that her student had much knowledge in the subject. Even so, there was one area which she doubted he could not explain.

"And what about the dinosaurs?"

"What about them?"

"The Bible says that the earth was created in six days, right?"

"Yes."

"And on the sixth day he created man, right?"

"Yes."

"And man was to have domain over all living things, right?"

"Yes."

"But we know that dinosaurs ruled the earth for millions of years. How could a weak and defenseless man have dominance over a 40 ton dinosaur?"

"How could he have domain over a lion or a tiger? That was the way that God intended the world to be. It never occurred because of man's original sin. The whole world changed with man's disobedience to God."

"That still doesn't explain the existence of dinosaurs. According to the creationist's theory of life, mankind has only been on this planet for about 10,000 years, right?"

"That sounds about right."

"Well, if God created the world for man - so that he could have dominance over it - and man was only created 10,000 years ago, how could the dinosaurs have been around for millions of years before?"

"Uh, I guess that's one thing I don't have an answer to. See, like I told you, I'm not an expert in this."

"Well," she said with a laugh as she arose from her desk, "you've certainly given me a lot to think about. Although I don't think we'll ever agree on this, Mr. Haggerty. But that's what this country is all about. We all have a right to our own opinion."

"That's true, Professor Montero," he answered as he also arose, "but I think it's a lot more than just an opinion."

"Meaning?"

"Well, if you believe in evolution then you can't believe in God. And if you don't believe in God, you won't believe in Jesus. And if you don't believe in Jesus you can't go to heaven."

"Mr. Haggerty," she said with a smile, "I certainly do appreciate your concern, but, like I said, we're not going to agree on this. I will, however, try to not mention evolution during my lectures. Or, if I do, I'll give equal time to the creation theory."

"Okay," he returned hesitantly, "I wish I could think of something else to say to convince you that the universe was created by God. But I appreciate you taking the time to talk to me."

"It has been an enlightening experience, Mr. Haggerty," she replied as they walked out of the classroom.

Cecilia Montero left her classroom and went hurriedly to her office. As intriguing as she found her conversation with Mr. Haggerty, she was glad it was over. She had begun to feel tired and lethargic again, and the pain under her ribs had gotten worse. She felt certain that her doctor's suspicion was correct - that the discomfort was caused by her gall bladder. Tomorrow's ultrasound test should confirm her suspicion. And, even though the surgery would certainly be no picnic, after the pain, fatigue, and nausea she had been experiencing the past few weeks, it would almost be welcome.

The next morning Cecilia Montero parked her car in the outpatient parking lot at Georgetown University Hospital. Since the test would be unobtrusive and pain free, she had declined a friend's offer to drive her. She had only to relax on the table while the radiologist viewed her digestive system. She applauded the achievements of modern medicine.

Before the procedure she asked the radiologist if he would be able to inform her of his findings. He stated that his directive was to provide the information only to her physician. The exam seemed to be taking more time than she had expected.

"So you can't tell me what you see?" she asked.

"Well, we're not supposed to. I will tell you though, I don't see anything wrong with your gall bladder."

"Hum," she stated. "Dr. Stanley was certain that was the problem. Do you see anything else wrong?"

"Well, it's not quite that simple. We take a picture of everything and then study them. We'll get the results to your doctor as soon as possible, and she'll go over it with you."

"That sounds kind of suspicious to me," she replied. "You don't have any idea of what the problem is?"

"I'm sorry, but that's all I can tell you."

The examination was soon over. Within fifteen minutes she was dressed and on her way home to her apartment in Bethesda, Maryland, unsure of whether she should be happy or worried. If it wasn't her gall bladder, what could the problem be? She had a friend who had experienced similar problems. The doctors were never able to diagnose its cause, and finally told her that they felt the pain was due to "irritable bowel syndrome", a condition in which the large intestine, for an unknown reason, but usually related to stress, goes into spasm. She decided that she must have the same problem. Her life was probably even more stressful than her friend's. She tried to put the issue out of her mind until she talked to her doctor.

The next morning her class ended at eleven o'clock. She intended to call her doctor when she returned to her office, however, upon checking her voice mail, found that she had a call from Dr. Stanley's office. Upon returning the call, she was informed by the secretary that Dr. Stanley had received the results of the test and wished to see her that afternoon.

"This seems awfully urgent. Is there some problem?" she asked.

"I really don't know," responded her secretary. "She probably just wants to see you because she knows how bad you've been feeling. So can you come in this afternoon?"

"Okay. My last class is over at three. How about three-thirty?"

"That'll be fine. We'll see you then."

She was now even more concerned than before. Why did her doctor wish to see her so soon? And why had the radiologist delivered the test results so quickly if there was no problem? She could do nothing but wait.

Somehow she managed to make it through her next class. She

did not know if her students realized she was not her normal self. They were probably so wrapped up in their own thoughts and problems that they noticed nothing.

Arriving at Dr. Stanley's waiting room at three-thirty, she only had a short wait before the nurse ushered into her office.

"So, Doctor, I don't have a bad gall bladder, huh?"

"No, it looks like your gall bladder is fine."

"But the way you rushed me in here the radiologist must have seen something, right?"

"Well, yes, there could be a problem."

"Okay," she returned as she took a deep breath, "What's the bad news?"

"Well, we're not certain how bad it is yet, but there seems to be a spot on your pancreas."

"A spot? You mean cancer?"

"I don't want to say that yet. It may be nothing more than a benign cyst, but we don't want to waste any time finding out. That's why I wanted you here so soon. We need to do another test to give us a better picture."

"What test?"

"A CAT scan with a biopsy. I have you scheduled for tomorrow morning at eight-thirty. Is that okay?"

"Yeah, I guess," she replied, her head still spinning. She felt tired and weak, as if all her energy had been sucked from her.

"Are you okay?" asked Dr. Stanley.

"I guess," she answered weakly, "This is just quite a shock."

The doctor removed a white plastic pack from her desk, shook it and handed it to Professor Montero.

"Here, put this on your head."

"What is it?"

"It's a chemical ice pack. It should help."

She did so as she leaned her head back. The doctor watched her for a few seconds.

"Do you want to lie down?" she asked.

"No thanks. I think this is helping."

She soon removed the pack from her head and turned back to the doctor.

"So this test will tell me if I have cancer of the pancreas?"

"Well, it will tell us what is there - but, yes, that is one possibility."

"And if so, that's like getting a death sentence, right?"

"Not necessarily. It depends on how far along it is. But let's take it one step at a time. I've had patients with the same symptoms and same test results who've had nothing but a cyst. Let's see what the test shows first."

"Well, I guess I have no choice."

Dr. Stanley reached into her desk and removed two small pills and handed them to her patient.

"Here, take these with you. It's a mild sedative. They'll help you sleep. Take one about an hour before bedtime and another in the middle of the night if you need it. But make sure you set your alarm in plenty of time to have the test done."

"Okay," she said absentmindedly. "Is this test painful?"

"It's uncomfortable. You'll be sedated so you will need someone to drive you home. Do you have someone?"

"Yes, I'll call a friend."

Cecelia sat in the chair for a few more minutes before she could gain enough energy to leave. Dr. Stanley informed her that she could have someone drive her home but she declined, saying she would be fine.

She arrived back at her apartment, absent-mindedly closed the door behind her and threw herself on the couch. For the next few minutes she lay staring at the ceiling, wondering why this was happening to her. Finally, with what renewed energy she had, she arose, walked to the telephone, and called her office. She checked her voice mail. She only had two messages, neither of which was important. She then called her department head to inform him that she would not be in the next day. To her relief she received his voice mail. She informed him that the test had shown nothing so she would have to take another. She saw no reason to give him the real details. She had no classes scheduled for the following day so no substitute would be necessary. And, hopefully, the test would show no serious problem, so there was no need to share her worry with others at this point.

She called her friend Marcie, a real estate agent. She prayed she would be home. She answered on the second ring. Although she had not talked to her in the past couple of days, Marcie was aware of the problems she had been having. She was not, however, prepared for the news her friend gave her.

"I'm sorry, Cecelia, but try to not worry too much yet. It's probably just a cist like the doctor said." she exclaimed. "I mean, you've always been the healthiest person I know."

"At least up until now."

Cecilia asked her if she could go with her to have the test, to which Marcie readily agreed. Somehow she made it through the remainder of the day. As instructed, she took the pill given her shortly before bedtime. Even with the pill she was afraid she would be awake all night. It was, however, only a short time before she was sleeping soundly.

Suddenly she was back in her childhood home near San Juan. Although it was easily recognizable, it had changed much. Instead of being a rundown house in one of San Juan's poorer neighborhoods, it was now a beautiful mansion. Out back, where the garden once grew, was now a large, dazzling swimming pool. Standing near the pool, laughing, eating, and drinking, were all the people she had known in her life. She saw her father - long since deceased - her mother, her brother, and all of her other relatives. Standing with them were all the friends from her childhood, as well as those from her adult life.

She soon found herself alone in the pool. The others waved to her as she swam back and forth. A feeling of peace and love spread over her. Then suddenly she began to sink, choking as she fought against the water. Her friends and relatives smiled and calmly waved as she fought to keep from going under. The harder she fought to stay afloat, the deeper she sank. Soon she felt her feet touch the bottom of the pool. Just as she was about to lose consciousness, a figure appeared in front of her - a beautiful young man in a white gown. His face was the most beautiful she had ever seen. He moved closer to her, put his mouth against hers and breathed air into her lungs. With a loving smile, he moved back and - as suddenly as he had appeared - he was gone. She could now breathe. As she began her journey to the top, she felt a joy and peace she had never known.

Cecelia sat up in bed, her clothes soaked with perspiration. It had been quite a dream. She wondered what it had meant. With the effects of the pill she did not ponder it long before falling back asleep.

They were at the clinic fifteen minutes before the test was to begin. The technician came out and took her into the lab area, and had her change into a gown. The radiologist came and greeted her as the technician positioned her on the table. He informed her that the test would take about twenty to thirty minutes. As was the case the day before, he told her that he would not be able to give her the results of the test. She would have to discuss that with her doctor.

She was placed on the bed of the CAT Scan and given and IV. She lay motionless, trying to not think of what the test might reveal. While the doctor told her the medication would only make her drowsy, she remembered nothing until the test was over.

She was finished with the test and back in recovery by nine-thirty. An hour later she was released and Marcie drove her home. They had lunch together, trying to avoid any discussion of Cecelia's health.

Soon Cecelia turned to her friend with a serious look. "Marcie, can I ask you a question?"

"Sure," answered Marcie.

"We've never really discussed this but - well, do you believe in God?"

"Well, it's not something I've given a great deal of thought to," she responded. "But yeah, I would like to think that there's a God somewhere. I guess this makes you really think about that, huh?"

"Yeah and - well, you know me - I've always been a strong believer in evolution and - well, to tell you the truth, I don't want to abandon my beliefs now just because of this. It would be like I've been living a lie all these years. But at the same time, what if I am wrong? If God really does exist and I haven't been living the right kind of life, I could be in real trouble if this is cancer."

"I'm sorry, Ciel, but I'm not the right person to talk to about something like that. I guess it's something I should think about, but I just haven't."

"Okay," she responded.

So that she would not have long to worry, Dr. Stanley had scheduled an appointment with her for the next morning. That would give the radiologists enough time to study the tests and get the results to her office. Marcie offered to cancel a closing on a house to accompany her, but Cecilia told her she would be fine. However, by the time she reached the doctor's office, she was already exhausted.

"Well, doctor," she began, "What's the word?"

Dr. Stanley removed her glasses, folded her hands, and leaned back in her chair. "I wish there was an easy way to do this, Ms. Montero, but there isn't. The test confirmed what I expected. You do have cancer of the pancreas. I'm terribly sorry."

Although she had thought she had prepared herself for this moment, actually hearing the words was like a blow to the stomach. She closed her eyes for a moment, hoping when she opened them it would be a bad dream.

"I'm only forty-one," she stated weakly after a long silence.

"I know," said Dr. Stanley.

Cecilia sat silently for a moment, staring at the floor. Suddenly she looked upward, remembering what the doctor had told her earlier.

"But you said that it might not be so bad - that it might not be a death sentence."

"Yes, I did," she returned reluctantly. "Unfortunately that was if we caught it at the early stage. I'm sorry to say that yours is already quite advanced. To be honest, I'm surprised your symptoms are not worse than they are."

"Well," said Cecilia with crack in her voice, "I always have had a high tolerance for pain. It's funny - I always thought that was good."

Dr. Stanley looked at her for a few seconds, then arose and took her by her arm, and walked with her to a nearby couch.

"Just rest here for a few minutes."

When she felt she was able to listen, Dr. Stanley explained to her what to expect in the few weeks, or perhaps months, that she had left. She told her what they would be able to do to make it easier on her. But then she spoke the words she always hated to say. "Mrs. Montero, I'm afraid, short of a miracle from God, there is no hope of a recovery."

Cecilia buried her face in her hands and began to sob.

"Is there someone I can call to come and be with you?"

"No, I'm afraid not. My best friend is tied up today, and I don't want to bother coworkers."

"Then I'll have someone drive you home."

The doctor gave her a prescription for medication, which would help relieve the effects of the disease, then called in a nurse and instructed her to drive her home. She informed Cecelia that someone would deliver her car later. As the nurse escorted her to the door, Dr. Stanley said the only thing there was left to say. "Mrs. Montero, I'm so sorry. We'll do everything possible to make things comfortable for you."

"Thank you," she said as the nurse helped her out the door. Dr. Stanley watched as they left her office.

———————

Cecelia Montero was still in a daze as the nurse helped her into her apartment. The nurse remained for a few minutes offering whatever assistance she could provide. Soon, however, Cecelia, stating that she would rather be alone, asked her to leave.

Her entire body ached. She couldn't believe this was happening to her. What had she done to deserve this? There had to be some mistake. That was it. These things happened often. There had been an error with the tests. But what about the sonogram? It had also shown something on her pancreas. Maybe it was wrong also. There were other tests. She would rest for a day, and then demand another test.

A short time later Marcie called. Through her tears, she told her the news.

"Cecilia, I'm so sorry. I'm just in shock. I don't know what to say. But I think you should have another test done or maybe have another doctor look at the results."

"That's what I was thinking. I'll call Dr. Stanley tomorrow. Right now I'm just too tired."

Marcie continued to tell her friend how sorry she was, and also insisted on coming by to check on her. Cecilia declined, stating that she was too tired and just wished to rest.

Their conversation ended with Marcie insisting that she come by the following day to see her. Cecilia then returned to the couch and lay down again. For the next few minutes she lie still, staring at the ceiling, her mind flashing to various scenes of her life. She was a young girl in Puerto Rico playing in the streets with her older brother; she was a young woman living with her aunt in Baltimore; she was receiving her degree in education from Johns Hopkins University; she was telling her boyfriend, Teddy, that she was too young to settle down - that she had to make a career for herself first.

That was the thing that seemed to bother her most - that she had never married or had a family. If she had, perhaps she would not feel so terribly alone now. No, she thought - that would probably make things even worse. For no one could share or even understand the loneliness she now felt. And, if she did have a family of her own, it would only increase the suffering. It was better this way.

But wait - this was still premature. The doctors could be wrong. It had happened before. Like she said, she would call and talk to other doctors - have another test done. There was still hope.

But for now, there was one other thing that had to be done. She had to let her boss know what was going on. She realized that, at least for now, there was no way she could return to work. She had to let him know what had happened. But what exactly should she tell him? No need to tell him she was going to die if it turned out not to be true. She decided to compromise - to tell him half the truth.

She waited until she knew Professor Laughton would be in his office. As much as she hated to discuss the matter with him, it was not the kind of message you leave on someone's voice mail. She informed him that the test was inconclusive - that it showed there might be a problem with her pancreas, but that it would be a few more days before they knew for certain. In this manner she would have time to talk to other doctors or have other tests done before she had to talk to him again. He offered his sympathy and support, and told her not to worry about her classes - the other faculty would cover for her. She told him that she wished him to only inform her students that she was ill and would be out for a while. She would contact him in a few days when she knew more.

Somehow she made it through the night, and the next morning Marcie came by and kept her company. They laughed and cried as they talked about the many times they had spent together. If only for a few minutes, it made her forget about her current situation.

After Marcie left, she called Dr. Stanley and questioned her about the accuracy of the radiologist's prognosis, and the possibility of having another doctor examine the results. She also asked if there might be other tests which were more accurate.

"Professor Montero," began Dr. Stanley, "I know this is difficult for you to accept - and I really wish I could give you a different answer - but there is no possibility of error. The clinic that did your test is the best - that's why I sent you there. And the doctors there are very careful - especially in a situation as critical as this. The cancer has already spread to other organs. But, just to satisfy your doubts, I will have another radiologist look at the results. But please, Professor, don't get your hopes up."

"I understand," she said. "But what about another test?"

"The only other thing we can do is surgery, and, to be honest, I don't think we should put you through that. It's risky in itself, and, in my opinion, it's only delaying things."

"Okay," she said. "I understand."

Dr. Stanley agreed to have the test results sent immediately to another radiologist. She again offered her sympathy for what she was going through.

The radiologist called Cecelia directly the next morning. From the tone of his voice, she knew immediately what the answer would be. He too offered his sympathy, and then confirmed what she already knew.

She could no longer delay the inevitable. She again called her boss and told him the bad news. He, like everyone else, could only offer his sympathy and prayers. She requested that he not tell her students or coworkers yet. She still did not know if she would return to work so wanted to delay the decision of informing them.

Still, it was a few more days before she finally accepted her situation. It was not, however, the doctors diagnosis which convinced her. She simply could no longer deny what was going on within her body. The nausea had gotten worse, as had the discomfort under her ribs. The pills helped some, but she hated taking them. Each one she swallowed was a confirmation of what she already knew. Three days later she called her boss again and told him there was no need to withhold the news from the faculty or students.

It was Saturday morning and she felt better than she had the previous few days. She decided, rather than sit around feeling sorry for herself, she would visit her office. The place would be deserted so she would have no questions to answer, nor be subjected to pitying eyes.

She parked her car in her parking space and walked to her office. The only person she encountered was the guard, whom she only recognized enough to say hello. It felt strange to be back at her desk - not because of the length of time she had been away, for it had only been slightly more than a week - but because it, like everything else, reminded her of what she would be leaving. She wiped a tear from her eye as she seated herself at her desk and began going through her incoming box.

There were the usual unimportant school memos and administrative notices, along with notes and cards from her colleagues and students. She glanced at them only long enough to see who they were from, then tossed them in a pile.

She soon noticed a large brown envelope with Professor Montero written in bold letters. She opened the envelope and removed the contents. Enclosed was a note attached to copies of newspaper and magazine articles. The note was from one of her students, Brian Haggerty. She read:

Professor Montero;
I'm sorry that you're not feeling well. I hope you're back soon. In the meantime I found a few articles related to our recent

conversation which I thought you might find interesting. Let me know what you think.

    Brian Haggerty

    The note was obviously written before he knew the seriousness of her condition. She glanced at the first article. Although the copy was faded, it was easily readable. It was written by a geologist who had studied Mt. St. Helen volcano a year after the eruption in 1980. She scanned the article only enough to understand the point he was making. The writer stated that if he had not known that the eruption had occurred the previous year, he would have been certain that the rock formations formed from the lava were thousands of years old. It had, in fact, completely changed his ideas of the age of the earth, which led to his rethinking his ideas on evolution and creation.

    The second article was copied from a book, obviously written by a creation scientist. It discussed the use of carbon dating to support evolution. The scientist explained that carbon dating could only be used on organic material and was therefore completely useless for estimating the age of rocks or minerals. He went on to explain that carbon dating could only be used to measure the age of organic material less than a few thousand years old. He explained that the age of fossils, therefore, was not measured by carbon dating, but was usually estimated by what life forms evolutionists believed to be alive during a certain period. In short, carbon dating could not be used as proof that life began millions of years ago as evolutionists claimed.

    The final article was one that had been copied from a national news magazine. It dealt with the pictures taken from the Hubble Space Telescope and how they contradicted the Big Bang Theory. The article explained that, if the universe were created as described in the Big Bang Theory, then all matter in the universe would be scattered symmetrically - as one would expect in any type of explosion. But the pictures of the universe taken from the Hubble

Telescope did not show that to be so. It did, in fact, show an ordered or planned universe. Upon seeing the pictures many scientists had, in fact, abandoned the Big Bang Theory.

Cecelia Montero smiled as she looked through the articles. What a nice kid Mr. Haggerty was. She folded the articles and put them in her purse, planning to read them in detail at a later time.

She spent the next hour going through her desk and identifying personal items she wished to remove. She put everything in a shopping bag she had brought with her, then, with a sigh, turned and studied the room before leaving. She realized it would probably be the last time she ever saw it.

The guard glanced briefly through her bag and nodded his approval. If he recognized her, he made no comment. Perhaps he knew who she was, and her condition, but felt too uncomfortable to say anything. It was just as well with her.

She arrived back at her apartment just before noon, made a sandwich and a bowl of soup, and ate in silence. Afterward she lay on the couch, determined to make a decision about something she had put off the last few days. She had to decide how she would spend the next few weeks - the last few weeks - of her life. She soon fell asleep. Two hours later, she was awakened by the ringing of the phone.

"Hi, Ceil," said Marcie. "How are you doing?"

"As well as can be expected, I guess."

"You feel up to going out to dinner?"

"I guess, if we make it early. I run out of steam by seven o'clock."

Marcie said she would pick her up at five but she declined, stating she would like to drive herself while she was still able. They agreed to meet at a favorite restaurant of theirs in North Arlington, about twenty minutes from her home.

They enjoyed their meal, sometimes laughing, sometimes crying, but continually talking about their many experiences together. They had known each other for ten years, since they were both teachers at George Mason University in Fairfax, Virginia. Cecilia had gone on to get her PhD., while her friend had decided to go into real estate. Over the years they had helped each other through many of life's problems, but Marcie was at a loss as how to help her friend now. All she could do was again tell her how sorry she was.

It was dusk when the two women exited the restaurant. Marcie asked her friend if she felt up to stopping at a nearby bar for a drink, but she declined. The two walked to the parking lot, hugged each other, and went their separate ways.

Cecelia started her car, turned on the headlights, and headed for home. She knew North Arlington quite well, having lived there many years earlier. She decided to take an alternate and more scenic route home, going through the exclusive neighborhood of McLean. She headed west on Lee Highway and turned down a side street which would take her to Old Dominion Boulevard, a direct route to McLean. It had been many years since she had been in the neighborhood, but it had changed very little.

It was not long before she realized that her memory was not as good as she thought, for the street and neighborhood were now unfamiliar. She did not worry; all she had to do was find a main street to get her bearings. She drove slowly, looking for a familiar sight. She soon noticed a sign which read *Bethlehem Bible Church*. Although there were no cars in the parking lot, a light came from inside. She decided to stop for directions.

It was a small but modern structure, which made it look more like an office building than a church. She pulled her car into a space near the entrance and walked inside.

"Hello," she called as she closed the door behind her. After receiving no answer, she repeated her call. She still got no response.

She looked down a darkened hallway which appeared to lead to the church's offices. She soon realized that the light in the building was coming from the sanctuary, which she walked into and repeated her greeting. Still she received no response. She stood at the entrance for a moment, then slowly walked down the aisle and seated herself in a pew near the center of the chamber. Sitting motionless, she looked behind the altar at a statue of Jesus, twisting in pain on the cross. She found herself asking the same question she had so many times before - does God really exist? She needed some sign - some proof that He was real. Then she did something she had not done since she was a child - she bowed her head to pray.

She prayed that God take away her cancer and make her whole again. She prayed for guidance and direction in how to handle her illness. And she prayed that he give her a sign to let her know He really existed. As she finished her prayer, she was startled by a nearby voice.

"Are you all right, sweetie?"

She looked up to see a gray-haired lady standing at the end of the pew.

"Oh, you startled me," she stated.

"I'm sorry, dear," returned the stranger, "but are you okay? You look pretty upset."

She started to tell her no - that she was fine, but she knew that would be a lie. She was far from being okay. She had heard that it is sometimes easier to talk to a stranger than someone you know.

"Do you work here?" asked Cecilia.

"I'm Ruth Carmichael. I'm with the church," she returned. "And you are...?"

"Cecilia Montero - Professor Cecelia Montero."

The lady moved closer and seated herself next to her.

"Well, Cecelia, why don't you tell me what is troubling you so?"

Cecelia took a deep breath and told her of her condition, frequently stopping to dry her eyes. When she had finished she turned to the stranger with a look of desperation.

"I'm so sorry, Cecelia. You have all my love. But I need to ask you a question dear. Are you a Christian?"

"Well, no, I guess not," she stammered. "I mean, I went to church when I was a little girl, but I've always had a problem trying to figure out if God really does exist. I'm not the type who can just accept something on faith. If God really did create the universe, then we should be able to see proof of His existence all around us."

"And you haven't been able to see that?" she asked.

"No, I guess I haven't," she said with a crack in her voice.

"And I guess that is a real concern with your current condition?"

"Yes, it is. I mean, I don't want to make a decision out of fear. And I don't want to give up the beliefs I've had all my life, but, if I'm wrong, I don't want to go to hell when I die either."

"What do you mean about making a decision out of fear?"

"Oh, I know what it means to be a Christian - that you have to believe in Jesus to be saved. But how can I believe in Jesus if I don't believe in God? And how can I believe in God when there is so much proof that He doesn't exist? There is just so much I don't understand. Like, if God does exist, why is there so much suffering in the world? And, if we were really created in His image, why is there so much evidence that we evolved from the lower life forms. I'm just so confused."

Mrs. Carmichael said nothing but displayed a Bible and began turning the pages. Cecelia was surprised, since she had not noticed her carrying a Bible when she sat down.

"My dear," she said, "I hate to tell you this, but the questions you are asking are not new or unexpected ones. But, at the same time, you, as a human, will never be able to totally understand God's plan. Let me illustrate by reading Isaiah chapter 55, verses eight and nine." She began to read; "For my thoughts are not your thoughts, neither are your ways my ways, saith the Lord. For as the heavens are higher than the earth, so are my ways higher than your ways and my thoughts higher than your thoughts."

"Wow," replied Cecilia as she again wiped a tear from her eyes, "I've never heard that."

"So you see, my dear, God knew that, with the intelligence He had given us, people would be questioning Him, but He also knew that we would never be able to fully understand. That's why He provided those words."

"That's really something," she replied. "But even so, there is still so much evidence in the world that contradicts the biblical explanation for creation. I really want to believe, but it's so difficult."

Mrs. Carmichael looked at her for a moment, then handed her the Bible.

"I want you to read something, dear."

"What is that?"

"Turn to the book of Job, chapter 40, beginning at verse 15," she instructed. "I don't know if you know anything about the book of Job, but basically it's about a man named Job who is questioning God and the wisdom of why He did things. God replies by asking him who he is to question His wisdom and His power. This is part of his reply."

"Okay," she agreed as she turned to the table of contents to find Job. She then began reading. "Behold now, behemoth, which I made with thee; he eateth grass as an ox. Lo now, his strength is in his loins, and his force is in the navel of his belly. He moveth his tail like a cedar: the sinews of his stones are wrapped together. His bones are as strong pieces of brass; his bones are like bars of iron. He is the chief of the ways of God: He that maketh him can make his sword to approach unto him. Surely the mountains bring him forth food, where all the beasts of the field play. He lieth in the shady trees, in the covert of the reed and fens. The shady trees cover him with their shadow; the willows of the brook compass him about. Behold he drinketh up a river, and hasteth not; he trusteth that he can draw up Jordan into his mouth. He taketh it with his eyes; his nose pierceth through snares."

After finishing the chapter she sat silently, trying to comprehend what she had read. Finally, she turned to her new friend.

"I'm not sure what this means."

"Think about it, dear. What kind of creature is so big that its tail is like a cedar tree? What kind of creature has bones like pieces of brass - like iron? And the part about him drinketh up a river and haseth not - the literal Greek translation says that although the river may rage, he is not disturbed. What kind of creature is so huge that flood waters pass it by?"

"Wow," she said as she began to understand. "A dinosaur?"

Mrs. Carmichael smiled and patted her on her hands.

"So this is saying that God created the dinosaurs," she continued. "I never knew the Bible made reference to dinosaurs."

"Yes, dear, most people don't. Besides showing Job the greatness of his power, I also believe God put that passage in the Bible for people of our times."

"Yes," she returned absentmindedly as she re-read the passage.

Her new friend looked at her warmly for a second, then arose and turned away.

"I have something I have to do. Will you wait here?"

"Sure," returned Cecilia.

Ruth turned and walked down the aisle. Cecilia continued reading the passage. How ironic that she had directed her to the passage about dinosaurs. When she had finished she again bowed her head to pray. She soon heard the footsteps of Mrs. Carmichael returning.

"You don't know how much.....," she began as she turned to face her friend. She stopped abruptly, however, when she realized the steps she heard were not those of Ruth but of a middle-aged man.

"Oh," she said as he walked toward her, "I thought you were Ruth."

"Ruth?" he inquired.

"Yes. She just went out for a minute."

"Well," he said as he stood at the end of the aisle, "before I ask you about Ruth, I'd like to know how you got in here?"

"How I got in here?" she returned in confusion, "I just walked in. Who are you?"

"I'm Terry Dunne, the church's pastor," he returned. "And I was just here an hour ago and turned off the lights and locked the door. So I'm still kind of confused as to how you got in here. And who is Ruth?"

"Mrs. Carmichael. She said she worked for the church. And I told you, the door was open so I just walked in. I guess Mrs. Carmichael had left the door open."

The pastor soon realized that the stranger was sincere and had no intentions of harming his church. He did, however, ask her to remain while he looked for her friend. He soon returned and seated himself near her.

"Well, there's no one else in the building now," he stated.

"Then I don't understand," she returned. "She just walked out a few seconds before you walked in."

The pastor asked Cecilia to explain exactly what had happened. She began telling him everything. She told him about her illness. She told him how she had seen the light coming from the church and had somehow been drawn inside. She told him how she had seated herself only to soon be joined by Mrs. Carmichael. And she told him about how her new friend had given her her Bible and instructed her to read the passage in Job. He took the Bible from her and looked through it.

"This is a nice Bible...kind of old, but very nice. It's strange, though...there's no name or information of any kind about who it belongs to."

"Well, I can assure you it's not mine. I haven't had a bible since I was..."

She stopped, embarrassed by her last remark. The pastor moved closer and put his hand on hers.

"Okay," he began, "the real important question here is are you all right? Did she help answer your questions?"

"Well, I was really enjoying talking to her, but we had just begun. There are so many things I need to know. I just need a sign that God really exists."

He looked at her for a moment, pondering what he should say. Soon, he began to speak.

"Cecilia, I want you to listen closely to what I have to say. This is a small church - I know every regular church member. There is no Ruth Carmichael associated with this church."

"I don't understand," she said.

"And there certainly is no Ruth Carmichael that works for the church. And, as I told you before, I locked the church and turned off all the lights less than an hour ago. When I got home I realized I had forgotten something so I had to come back."

"What does this mean?" she asked.

"You said you wanted a sign that God really exists. I think you got it."

"What!" she exclaimed, trying to comprehend what he was saying. "You mean Ruth was..."

"I'm not sure who or what Ruth was, but I feel certain that she was sent from God. The real important question is did she convince you that He really exists?"

"Well, I don't know," she said in confusion. "We...we had just begun talking."

"Listen to me Cecilia," he said forcefully. "It's time for you to quit this foolishness. You'll never be able to have every question answered. There's only one way to assure your salvation, and I think you know what that is. Do you want to ask Jesus to come into your life?"

She began to cry uncontrollably. He moved closer and wrapped his arms around her. The light shone dimly through the church window as the pastor prayed with her.

It was a day as perfect as could be imagined in the Washington, D.C. area. It was early May and the flowers brought new life to the American University campus. Brian Haggerty walked slowly to his dormitory, taking time to enjoy the sunshine. After entering the building, he stopped and removed the mail from his mailbox. It was the usual - credit card applications, campus notices, bills, etc.

However, one letter caught his eye. There was no name, but the return address showed it had come from Puerto Rico. He tore it open and began to read:

> Dear Mr. Haggerty;
> You are probably surprised to get a letter from me, but I wanted to thank you for everything you've done for me. Please tell all the students that I'm sorry for leaving without talking to them, but, as I'm sure you will understand, it's been very difficult accepting my situation. I'm doing fine at the present, although that could change at any time. As you can see from the address, I'm back in Puerto Rico. I'm living with my mother. My brother and his family are nearby, so I get to see them almost every day. I want to thank you for the conversation we had a few weeks ago. I'm sure you thought I disregarded everything that you said, but that wasn't the case. Although it took a long time, and a little intervention by God, I now understand. So, I just wanted to let you know not to worry about me. I would still prefer not to be in the situation I'm in, but at least now I know where I will spend eternity. Thanks again for your concern and for sharing your beliefs.
>
> Yours in Christ
> Cecilia Montero
>
> P.S.: Next time you have a conversation with someone like myself about dinosaurs, you might want to read them Job, chapter 40, verses 15 through 24.

ONE TO ANOTHER

The Boeing 757 pulled to a stop at gate 17 of Tampa International Airport. Immediately the baggage crew pulled open the cargo bay of the huge aircraft and began transferring the baggage to the awaiting carts. Howard Taylor, one of the younger members of the crew, worked hurriedly to unload the plane. Since it was the last plane of his shift, the sooner it was empty, the sooner he could head for home. Even though his work was physically demanding, he would not change it for any other. The pay was good, he got to work in the outdoors, which he loved, and he took great pride in the fact that - because of the job - he was in better shape than ninety percent of the men he knew. Although his muscles ached, it was a good ache - the kind that would soon go away with a hot shower and a few minutes rest.

Soon the belly of the plane was emptied and the crew headed for the hanger. Tory Lewis, one of the more experienced members of the crew, walked over to Howard and slapped him on the back.

"So, Howie," he said, "you still bowling with us tonight?"

"I said I was, didn't I?" answered Howard.

"Well, I just thought your little misses might not like it. You did get permission, didn't you?"

"Hey, I told you, I don't need permission. I'll be there. You just be ready to pay me that ten bucks when I beat your tail."

Tory roared with laughter, slapped him on the back once more, and walked away.

It was six-fifteen when Howie signed out and walked to his pick-up in the parking lot. He pulled onto Dale Mabry Boulevard and headed north. He soon turned eastward on Hillsborough Avenue. Fifteen minutes later he pulled into the driveway of his house in north Tampa - a small, three-bedroom rambler. It was located in an older, middle-class neighborhood. He hoped to someday move to a larger home in a better neighborhood, but for now this was adequate. He felt proud that, at age twenty-nine, he owned any type of house.

He parked his truck behind his wife's Dodge Neon and walked into the kitchen. His wife, LuAnn, was putting dinner on the table.

"Hey, babe," he said, smacking her on the fanny.

"Hi," she answered, turning to gave him a quick kiss.

"How was your day?" he asked.

"Not bad. How was yours?"

"About the same."

He washed his hands, poured himself a glass of tea, then walked into the living room. His eight-year old daughter, Tina, sat on the floor watching cartoons.

"Hi, Princess," he said.

"Hi, Daddy," she answered without looking up.

"Did you have a good day in school?"

"It was all right. We only have six weeks left. I'll be glad when it's summer."

"Hey, we live in Florida. It's summer all the time."

"You know what I mean, Daddy," she answered with a giggle.

"Where's your brother?"

"In his room, probably playing a computer game."

"Dinner is ready," called LuAnn from the kitchen.

"Go get Travis for dinner," said Howie.

Tina ran to the bedroom and soon returned with her six year-old brother. The four sat down to eat. They talked randomly about the events of the day as they enjoyed their meal. When done, Howie went to the bathroom and showered as LuAnn cleaned the kitchen. After dressing, Howie returned to the living room where his wife sat on the couch, paging through *Southern Living* magazine.

"Where are the kids?" he asked.

"Out back playing," she answered

The tone of her voice told him something was bothering her.

"What's wrong?" he asked.

"Are you still going bowling tonight?"

"Didn't we already have this conversation? I told you I was, didn't I. You got that Jackson girl to come by and watch the kids, didn't you?"

"Yes."

"Then I don't understand the problem. You know how to get to the hospital, don't you?"

"Don't be a smart aleck," she answered.

"Okay, honey," he said as he sat in a chair facing her, "I don't understand why this is such a big deal. You just go down to the hospital and visit your uncle for a few minutes. You take him a magazine and you tell him you're glad the operation went okay. Then you talk for a while and you leave."

"Howie, you know how much I hate doing things like this. You know how I hate hospitals. I don't ask you for much but I really would like you to go with me."

"Lou, I don't even know your uncle that well. I wouldn't know what to say."

"You wouldn't be doing it for him - you'd be doing it for me."

"I told you, honey, I already promised the guys I would be there. It's too late to get a sub now."

"It wouldn't have been too late when I first asked you."

Howie shook his head and arose from the chair.

"You know what I think your problem is, Lou?"

"No," she answered sarcastically, "why don't you tell me?"

"You don't appreciate me. I bring home a good paycheck. I don't drink - other than an occasional beer. I don't do drugs. I don't chase other women. I don't gamble. And I don't slap you around. I would think you would be grateful to have a man like me."

"Yeah, you're great. It's just too bad that you put me and the kids last in everything you do."

"Dammit, woman," he returned through clenched teeth, "as far as I know, I'm still head of this family, and I'm getting pretty tired of you questioning everything I do. Now I'm going bowling and that's that. I'll see you when I get home."

He stormed out the door. She heard the roar of his truck pulling away. She rubbed a tear from her eye, put the magazine aside, and walked to the yard to get her children.

———————

Howie turned onto Hillsborough Avenue once more and headed west. He was soon at the bowling alley in the Town & Country neighborhood. Most of the men from his team were already there, waiting at the bar. Tory raised his beer to greet him. "Get a beer and put on your shoes, or put on your shoes and get a beer."

Howie set his bowling ball on the floor, took his shoes from their bag, and put them on. When finished, he seated himself beside his co-workers and ordered a beer. They talked and joked while waiting for the final member of the team to arrive. Once he appeared they left the bar and walked to their assigned lane.

Although still upset over the argument with his wife, Howie did not wish to discuss it with the other members of the team. He knew that, once aware of the situation, the evening would be spent teasing and harassing him. He only wished Lou would be more understanding. He had a tough and demanding job, and his time with his friends was his only means of letting off steam. He felt that he contributed more than his share to their marriage. He brought home a paycheck while his wife stayed home taking it easy. He took care of the cars and made repairs around the house when needed. All she had to do was cook, clean, and take care of the children. And she had been complaining even more about that lately. She was often asking him to go to a meeting at the school - even after he had put in a long and tiresome day. He didn't know what was bothering her, but he hoped she'd get it resolved soon.

By the end of the second game, the effects of the alcohol were noticeable. The guys were more jovial - slapping each other high - fives for whatever reason they could invent. They talked and joked among themselves as they waited for the scores from the second game to be entered. Soon, one of the team members, Frank, turned to Howie with a question. "So Howie, me and Buddy and Tory are going fishing down to Lake Okeechobee this weekend. You want to come?"

"For how long?"

"Leaving early Saturday and coming back Sunday evening. You're not working this weekend, are you?"

"No," he answered slowly, "but I don't think I better do it. I got a lot of things to do around the house."

"That means he don't want to get on the wrong side of his misses," laughed Tory.

"That don't have nothing to do with it," Howie protested. "If I wanted to go, I'd go. I just got other things to do."

"Course I can't blame him," continued Tory. "That sure is a cute little lady he's got. He wouldn't want her withholding any of her favors, if you know what I mean."

Howie felt his blood pressure rise. Not only was he irritated about Tory's comment on how cute his wife was - even though it was true - but it also bothered him for the men to think he was controlled by her. He also knew that if he let Tory know that he was getting to him it would only make it worse.

"Well, you guys believe what you want," he said, acting as

unconcerned as possible.

"Don't let Tory get to you," said Ben, the more compassionate member of the team. "You know he's just trying to get you riled."

"Yeah, I know."

"If he knew so much about women he would still be married - to at least one of his three wives."

It was now Tory's turn to become irritated as the others laughed.

"Well you all go ahead and laugh, but I do know a few things about women and marriage," he said.

"Like what?" asked Frank.

"Like the thing that all these *women libbers* don't want you to know - that the man is supposed to be the head of the family. They believe that a man and his wife are supposed to share everything - that a marriage is a democracy. Well, hell, that's the problem with half the marriages in this country today. Women are going against what God intended."

"What God intended?" repeated Ben as the others shook their heads at Tory's remark.

"Sure," returned Tory seriously. "That's what the Bible says - that the man is the head of the family and that he is supposed to rule over the woman."

"What do you know about the Bible?" asked Howie.

"I know more than you think I do. My uncle was a preacher. I've been to church a few times in my life. And when I was married the first time, I had to go to pre-marriage counseling. The preacher even showed us where it said in the Bible that the woman was to submit herself unto her husband."

"I guess none of your wives believed that, huh?" asked Ben.

"Well, I'll tell you what, son," he continued, "I'd rather be sleeping by myself and having fun here with my buddies than with a woman that was always complaining and never appreciated anything that I did."

The conversation soon died down, and the group's attention was refocused on the game. Howie, however, silently contemplated what had been said. Before leaving, he turned and informed Frank that he would be joining them on their upcoming fishing trip.

As usual, Howie arrived home at six-fifteen the following evening. By six-forty-five he and his family had finished dinner. He sat on the sofa listening to the evening news as he read through the day's mail. His wife cleared the table and placed the dishes in the dishwasher. Afterward, she went into Tina's room where she and her brother had been playing. The three soon returned to the living room. Howie looked up to see his wife with her purse in her hand.

"Are you all going somewhere?" he asked.

"To our school, Daddy," responded Tina.

"Oh," he responded to his daughter but looking at his wife, "your play is tonight? Why didn't someone remind me?"

"We did," said LuAnn firmly. "Last week, and again on Sunday."

"Are you going to go, Daddy?" asked Tina.

He looked irritably at his wife, but continued to speak to his daughter.

"I don't know, Honey," he said. "I haven't even taken a shower yet. It would be over before I got there."

"No it won't," she insisted. "It doesn't start until eight o'clock. I just have to be there early."

"Well, I don't think so, honey. Daddy's pretty tired tonight and I have to go in early in the morning. How about if I catch your next play?"

"We understand," said LuAnn. "We know you don't like to stay out too late."

Howie felt his blood pressure rise. He knew his wife was referring to his previous night's bowling. He only hoped the children did not pick up on it. For their sake, he felt it best to say nothing.

"We better go, kids," she continued. "We don't want to be late."

The three hurried out the door and into the car. Howie took time from examining the mail to watch them drive away. He was irritated with his wife as well as himself. Despite what she had thought, he had truly forgotten the play was tonight. She could have reminded him when he got home. He was the one who had worked all day. He had many things on his mind. He thought for a moment about showering and driving to the school, but soon dismissed the idea. Even though his wife thought it to be an excuse, he was truly tired. But even more than that, if he did so, it would appear that he had only given in to appease his wife. He could not do that. It was time that she realized that he was the head of the family. He drank his iced tea and stared blankly at the TV.

It was the following evening - Thursday - before he told his wife that he was going fishing for the weekend. To his surprise, she offered no complaint. She only asked when they would be returning.

Howie arose before five o'clock Saturday morning. Having packed his fishing gear the night before, there was little to do while awaiting his friends. He ate a bowl of cereal, then quickly shaved, showered, and brushed his teeth. By five-thirty he was ready to leave. He quietly looked into the children's bedrooms before leaving. Both were sleeping soundly. He then returned to his bedroom where his wife also lay sleeping - or at least pretending to be. He bent over and kissed her on the check, then quietly left the room.

He only had a short wait before his friends arrived. Soon, Buddy's Chevy Blazer turned into the driveway. They quickly exited and helped Howie load his gear into the back of the vehicle. First daylight had just begun to break as they turned onto Route 60 heading east. By eight o'clock the foursome had arrived at their campsite. Tory complained repeatedly that they had already missed the best part of the day for fishing. The others countered that they would never arise at three o'clock to go fishing. They were, as they liked to call themselves, "gentle fishermen".

By nine o'clock the group had set up camp and shoved off in their rented boat. They fished, drank beer, and joked until lunch time. They returned to camp long enough to wash away the smell of fish before driving to a nearby diner for lunch. Afternoon found them lying in the tent, each sleeping soundly.

The rest of the weekend was spent similarly - fishing, drinking beer, and telling jokes. Although this had always been the environment Howie loved most - enjoying the great outdoors with his buddies - for a reason unknown to him, he found it difficult to relax. He went through all the motions of having a good time - he laughed at all the right times, told his share of lurid stories, and razzed the other members of the group as men alone are expected to do. But something was different about this trip. He had a gnawing feeling that something was wrong. He first thought it was due to the recent arguments with his wife, but he soon dismissed that idea. This was not the first time they had fought, nor was it the first time they had argued before he went away. He soon tried to dismiss the feeling and concentrated on enjoying the weekend.

The group left the campsite at six o'clock Sunday evening. The return trip was much quieter than the one going down. Some members were tired from the busy weekend. Others had simply run out of witticisms. For Howie, it was just as well. He felt physically and emotionally drained, and was glad to be going home.

It was half past eight when the Blazer pulled into his driveway. Howie quickly removed his gear from the rear of the vehicle. Since his family did not enjoy fish, he gave his weekend's catch to Frank. He waved good-bye as the men pulled out of his driveway.

He was irritated to see that LuAnn had closed the garage door - especially when she knew he would be returning home soon. He would now have to open it from inside before he could store his camping gear.

He was immediately struck by the quietness of the house as he entered the kitchen. Only one light was on in the living room. He surmised that everyone must be in the bedroom. He walked slowly down the hall, calling the names of his wife and children. He got no response. He looked into the children's bedrooms, but they were dark and empty. He then walked into the master bedroom, but it, too, was empty. He returned to the living room and stood silently, wondering where they might be.

He told himself it was silly to be concerned. LuAnn had just taken them out for ice cream. They would be back soon. But then it was unlike his wife to have the kids out so late on a school night. Although he was concerned, he decided to do nothing. He went into the garage and opened the door then placed his gear onto a storage shelf.

By nine o'clock his family still had not returned home. He picked up the phone to begin calling friends, then placed it back down. He didn't want to appear too worried or too emotional. He would wait a few minutes longer.

Fifteen minutes later, however, he was certain something was wrong. His wife would never have the children out so late on a Sunday night. He began calling their friends. Sounding as unconcerned as possible, he asked if they knew where LuAnn might be. No one did. Finally, he dialed the number of LuAnn's sister, Loretta. He had saved her until last, not because she was less likely to know his wife's whereabouts, but because he did not enjoy speaking to her.

Loretta's husband, Jacob, answered the phone. Howie explained that he was getting a little concerned because his wife and the kids were out so late. He asked Jacob if he knew where they might be. There was a long silence before he responded. "Well, yeah," he answered, "we know where they are. They're over here."

"Oh, well, good," said Howie. "I hope she's planning on leaving soon - it's getting late. Can I talk to her?"

"Well," continued Jacob deliberately, "Lou says she doesn't want to talk right now, Howie."

"What are you talking about, Jacob? What's going on over there?"

"Well, Howie, I guess what she's saying is that she's not coming home. I don't know how else to say it."

"She's not coming home!" he shouted. "What the hell is she talking about?"

"I guess she's upset about something, Howie. I don't know - I'm just telling you what she said. I don't know any more than that."

"Well, that's great. Tell her I want to talk to her - now."

"She said she will not talk to you tonight. She said you can come by tomorrow when the kids are in school if you want."

"Tomorrow! I have to work tomorrow. I want to know what this is all about. We have one or two little arguments and she takes my kids and splits. What kind of a woman is that?"

"Look, Howie," said Jacob, "I can't tell you more than that. Now I think you need to just try and calm down and talk to her tomorrow. Then maybe you two can get this thing all straightened out."

Howie paused for a moment. As upset as he was, there was no reason to take it out on Jacob. They had always had a decent relationship.

"All right," he said. "Tell her I'll try to get off early tomorrow and come by. I'll give her a call in the morning."

"Okay," said Jacob. "I'm sorry about this, Howie. I don't know what else to say."

"Thanks, Jacob. I appreciate that. And I appreciate you letting them stay there until we can get this straightened out."

"Sure thing," he said before hanging up.

Howie slowly hung up the phone and stared blankly at the floor. How could his wife do such a thing to him? This was another of her half-thought-out ideas, which she would soon realize was a mistake. How could she expect to take care of two young children when she didn't even have a job? Did she expect to live with her sister forever? And, possibly the biggest question, what was she so upset about that she would do such a thing?

He sat for a few minutes, further pondering her actions. Then, after looking at his watch, rose and walked hurriedly out the door, got into his pick-up and quickly drove away.

———————

It was almost ten o'clock when the doorbell rang at Jacob and Loretta Bowling's house. Before he went to the door, Jacob knew who it must be.

"Hey, Howie," he said. "I can't say I'm really surprised to see you."

"I'm sorry, Jacob. I just have to talk to LuAnn tonight. Is she still awake?"

"I really don't know. Her and Loretta have been up in her sewing room most of the evening. But she told me that she won't talk to you tonight."

"I don't know what the difference is between tonight and tomorrow. She's got to talk to me anyway."

"I don't know what to tell you, Howie. I'm in the middle here. I just know....."

As he spoke, the door opened wider to reveal his wife.

"It's okay, Jacob," she said. He looked at the two for a second before walking away.

LuAnn walked onto the porch, closing the door behind her. The two stared at each other in silence, each waiting for the other to begin. Finally Luann said, "Let's sit on the swing."

They walked to the end of the porch and seated themselves on the swing. LuAnn sat on the corner, turning to face her husband.

"So, what is this all about?"

"I think that is the point."

"Huh? You're not even making any sense."

"The point is that you don't even know what this is all about. You don't have a clue."

"No, I really don't. I mean - I know we've had a few fights lately - and I know I'm a little thoughtless sometimes, but I can't think of anything I've done that would lead you to do something like this."

"And again, that's the point. You don't know why I am so upset because you don't ever think of me first - or the kids either, for that matter. Basically, what you want is to be a single man with a family. You want to have your work, your buddies, your sports, your hobbies. You think that as long as you pay the bills and do a few repairs around the house that you are a good husband and father."

"That's what this is about? That I don't spend enough time with you and the kids? That I don't put you first in everything?"

"See, you still don't understand. You make it sound so trivial. I want a husband who loves me and treats me with respect. And, yes, I want a husband who puts me first once in a while - who understands my needs. And I want my kids to have a father that is always there for them - that loves them but is also there to discipline them when they need it. I can't take this feeling anymore that we're imposing on you every time I ask you to do something. That's the real purpose of being married - to have someone that will always be there for you - that will always put you first."

He sat silently, shaking his head. She waited for him to speak, but he said nothing. Even without a response from him, she could see that her words had little meaning.

"Well, let's hear it," she said. "You're going to say it sooner or later so it might as well be now."

He looked at her thoughtfully for a while longer before speaking.

"Okay. What I hear you saying is that you depend on me to do everything. I have to bring home a paycheck, make all the repairs on the house and car, discipline the children when they need it, plus be a counselor to you when you're feeling depressed. And then I'm not even allowed to have any time to myself to let off some steam."

"I'm sorry you have it so rough, Howie. If you...."

"I let you have your say," he interrupted, "now let me have mine."

"Okay."

"It's obvious that we have a difference of opinion of what a husband should be. You want a sensitive, tender, emotional man who you can tell all your secrets to and who will share all your fears and dreams. Well I think a man should be strong and tough - the leader of the family - the decision maker. Someone who..."

"Is this the part," she interrupted, "about how the Bible says a man is supposed to be the head of the family?"

"Well, you laugh at that Lou, and I ain't saying I'm the most religious guy in the world, but I do have certain beliefs, and that's one. I've heard that since I was a little boy in Sunday School. The problem is that all this women's lib stuff has led you to believe that the woman should be the head of the family."

"Howie," she said as shook her head, "It's useless to talk to you. No matter what I say I can't make you understand. I'm tired and I'm going to bed."

She arose and walked toward the door. He wanted to grab her - to shake some sense into her - but he did not. But he had one more thing to say before she left.

"You know, you only thought about yourself when you did this. You haven't even thought about what this is doing to the kids."

"No, you're wrong," she answered sharply. "I am thinking of them most of all."

He arose and angrily moved toward her.

"So now you're saying that my kids are better off without me?"

"I'm saying that I don't want my son to believe that this is the way to treat a wife, and I don't want my daughter to believe that this is what she has to look forward to. So if this is what it takes, then so be it."

"Well, ain't that nice of you, Lou. I appreciate you going to all this trouble to show me the way. How can I ever repay you?"

"Perhaps I can make it more clear to you Howie," she said with fire in her eyes. "When I told the kids that we would not be living together for awhile, do you know what Travis said? He didn't say how much he would miss his father. He didn't ask if you would still be able to play ball together - maybe because you never spend time with him anyway. You know what he asked? He wanted to know if you would still remember his name. Does that bring it home, Howie? Your son worries that you won't remember his name."

With the last statement, she opened the door and started inside. He stood in silence, trying to think of the right response to her remark. None came. She looked back at him for one brief second, then went inside and pulled the door behind her.

The next few days were very difficult for Howie. The feelings of loneliness and despair were at times almost unbearable. He never would have guessed that being separated from his family would have such a devastating affect on him. He had thought himself to be much stronger. Not that he had ever wondered what it would be like to be separated. Even with all the arguments he and LuAnn had had over the years, he had never seriously considered the thought of separation. And he was still in shock to discover that she had the determination to leave him. He thought he knew her so well, and now this. He still hoped, however, that she would soon come to her senses.

As devastated as he was, he was determined that none of his friends or co-workers would know. The last thing that he needed was advice or comments from people like Tory. Hopefully, things would return to normal soon, and he could put this whole nightmare behind him. All he had to do was to keep pretending everything was normal for a few more days until he and Lou could work out their differences.

The worst part was coming home to an empty house. He had never realized how much it meant to him to have his wife and kids home waiting for him. As much as he hated to admit it, perhaps some of the things that Lou had said were right. Perhaps he had been more thoughtless and insensitive than he realized. That, then, was the answer - to tell her that she was right - that he would really try to be more thoughtful and would spend more time with them. As long as she felt her actions had been justified, and that he saw her point of view, she would return home.

It had only been four days since she had left. He had talked to her only once since that time. He knew she had been going by the house to pick up clothing while he was at work, but he said nothing. He hoped by now, after she had had a few days to think about things, she would be more ready to listen to reason.

He waited until he knew the kids would be asleep before he called her. His sister-in-law answered the phone. She was cold but polite. He waited nervously for his wife to come to the phone.

"Hey, Lou," he said.

"Hi, Howie," she answered. "How've you been?"

"Not bad. How are you?"

"Okay."

"How are the kids?"

"They're fine. They are pretty anxious for school to be out."

"Right."

He paused for a second to collect his thoughts.

"Listen, Lou," he said, "I've been thinking a lot about some of the things you've said and - well, how do I say this. Well, I guess you're right about a lot of things. I guess I'm a lot more thoughtless than I realized. And - well damn it Lou, I miss you and the kids and I want you to come home."

He waited for what seemed to be an eternity for her response.

"Well, Howie," she said, "that's nice to hear. I really am glad to hear you say that, but I don't think I can come home just yet."

"I don't understand. I'm not playing a game. You know I don't say things if I don't mean them. It's not easy for me to say that I was wrong about something. And I'll try to be more thoughtful and considerate."

"Howie, I don't think it's as simple as that. I do appreciate what you are saying, but - well, to be blunt, I don't think it's possible for a person to change in just a few days. Oh, I think things would be fine for a while, but I believe we would be right back where we started in a couple of months."

"Well, I don't know what I'm supposed to do," he said, through clenched teeth. "I've agreed with you; I've told you what you want to hear; I've said I will try to change, and that's still not enough. What is it that you want?"

"Howie, for the past ten years I've put your needs first. We could only do something together if you didn't have a ball game or weren't going fishing or hunting. You were always too tired to do anything I wanted, but I don't think you've ever turned down one of your friends when they needed help. And, for almost as long, I've seen you treat our children the same way. They've learned to not even ask you to spend time with them. And only now, after your pride has been hurt and you're feeling lonely, do you tell me you were wrong. I'm sorry, Howie, but it's going to take a little more than that."

"Okay, Lou," he said with a deep sigh, "what can I do?"

"I really don't know, Howie. I just need a little more time. It's only been a few days, you know."

"In the meantime how are you going to get by? We haven't even talked about finances yet, you know."

"Yes, and I guess we'll have to talk about it if it comes to that. But, for the time being, I'm going to find a job. It's something I have been thinking about anyway."

"A job? What will you do? You haven't worked since we got married."

"I know, but I still think I have a few things to offer. As a matter of fact I have an interview with the Postal Service next Wednesday."

"Wow. Okay, Lou, I don't know what else to say. I'll leave the next step up to you. I just want you to know that I love you. No matter what else you think, you know that I've always loved you and have always been faithful."

He heard her muffled sobs. He was glad to know that he still evoked such a response. Even so, he was afraid to ask the next question.

"I guess next you're going to tell me that you no longer love me?"

"I don't know how to answer that, Howie. I'm not saying that I don't love you, but I don't think I can tell you that I do right now, either. I'm just really confused. I just need a little time."

"Okay," he answered.

He said good-bye to his wife and slowly hung up the phone. He sat silently, wondering how his life could have been torn apart in such a short period of time. After a few minutes he arose, locked the doors, and turned off the lights. He silently slid into bed, alone. He had never felt so lonely.

―――――――――

Howie made arrangements with LuAnn to pick up the kids on Saturday. He felt both resentment and embarrassment as he drove to his sister-in-law's house to pick up his children. Their uneasiness was also evident as they entered his truck. It was with some shame that he realized that this was the first time in recent memory that he had been alone with them.

The trio spent most of the day at Busch Gardens amusement park. The children soon forgot their uncomfortable situation - or at least appeared to - and enjoyed the rides. Howie was surprised how quickly the day ended.

He did not attempt to discuss matters with LuAnn when they

returned. Besides being too weary to discuss the situation again, he felt that it would be fruitless to do so. As difficult as it was for him, he felt he had no choice but to wait for Lou to take the next step.

Time seemed to be frozen as he moved through the next few days. He still had told no one of his situation. He felt that he had put up a good front at work, so that no one was suspicious that something was wrong. Luckily, the men he worked with did not often discuss personal or family matters. At first he had been grateful for that fact, but lately he had begun to wish that someone would ask him if everything was okay. But no one did, and he somehow managed to get through the week with at least part of his sanity intact.

It was Tuesday - bowling night once again. Last week had not been so bad. Tory had not been in attendance due to a sprained wrist, and the rest of the group had been much more civil without him. Tonight would be different. He would be back, and probably attempting to make up for lost harassment time. Howie was concerned that the group would learn that Lou had left him. He was also concerned about what he would do if Tory made one of his infamous statements about women and marriage. For that reason, he thought momentarily about canceling for the night. Finally, he decided against it. He would have to deal with the problem sooner or later, so it might as well be now. And, besides, he did not wish to sit at home again, thinking about his situation.

As usual, his friends were at the bar when he arrived. He ordered a draft beer and joined them. They spent the next few minutes joking and teasing each other. The announcement soon came that the lanes were ready. The group left the bar and seated themselves around the scorer's table.

As Howie expected, it was not long before Tory began his attempt to uncover what had been bothering him.

"So, Howie, buddy," he began as he seated himself next to him on the bench, "you've been awful quiet lately. Is everything okay?"

"What? Oh yeah, sure. I hadn't noticed. I guess I've just been a little tired. Maybe I got a cold coming on or something."

"You sure everything's okay? I mean we're your buddies here. If something's wrong maybe we can help."

"Oh, no, everything's fine," he answered, hoping he would drop the subject.

"Okay, just remember, we're here."

Although Tory let the subject drop, Howie knew that he did not believe him. He only hoped that it would be the last he heard of it that evening.

The first game ended soon. As was their routine, the rest of the group sat at a nearby table waiting for Ben to turn in the scores. Frank soon turned to Howie. "Howie, you never said how your misses acted when we got back from our fishing trip. Was she upset?"

Howie was irritated at the question, and even more irritated at the timing. Why had he not brought up the subject last week? Had he intentionally waited until Tory returned so that they could question him together?

"No, not really," he answered. "I mean I guess she was a little irritated that I was gone all weekend, but she soon got over it."

"Yeah, I understand," said Frank. "So was mine."

Howie waited for Tory to say something, but he made no comment, and Frank let the matter drop. Perhaps he was too suspicious in thinking they were plotting together to find out what was bothering him.

By half past nine, most of the teams had completed their final game. Howie's team had finished and now sat waiting for the others to complete their game so the final scoring could be tallied. Soon Ben turned to the others.

"Gang, to celebrate another fantastic season, my wife has suggested that we all get together at our house this Saturday for a cookout. Can you all make it?"

There was almost unanimous agreement from the group. Everyone agreed that they could be there - except for Howie who had made no comment.

"What about you, Howie?" Ben asked. "Can you all make it?"

"I don't think so. My wife made plans with her family. Sorry."

"Now what could be more important than a cookout with your best buddies?" asked Tory.

"I don't remember," he stammered. "I'm sure she told me but I don't remember what it was."

He wondered if they were suspicious of his statement. He felt as if they were all staring at him, questioning everything he said.

"Well," said Tory, "why don't you just tell her to postpone it? It's not often that we get a chance to get together like this."

"No," said Howie, as calmly as possible, "I can't tell her to cancel her plans. Sorry guys."

They nodded their understanding. Howie sat silently for a moment, wondering what they were thinking. He started to announce that he had to leave, but then changed his mind. As much as he disliked what he was about to do, he knew that he could no longer live a lie.

"Guys," he said seriously, "There's something I need to tell you. We don't really have plans for Saturday. The truth is - well, Lou and I aren't living together. We haven't been for over a week."

In unison, the members of the group began to express their surprise and sympathy. As they did so, a mixture of emotions swept over Howie - relief, embarrassment, and even a small degree of fear. He was relieved that he would no longer have to lie to his friends; he was embarrassed to admit his marriage was a failure; and he was afraid that their questions would now uncover the rest of his secret - that his wife had suddenly and unknowingly left him.

"That's too bad," said Frank.

"I'm really sorry, man," said Buddy. "That's a real bummer."

"Yeah," said Tory, somewhat distant, "that's a shame."

"When did this happen?" asked Buddy.

"Just after we got back from fishing. But I guess it's been coming a long time."

"Do you think this is permanent?" asked Frank.

"I don't know yet," he answered, "it's too early to tell. I'm just taking it one day at a time."

The men could see the pain in Howie's face as he spoke of his separation. They did not know if they should pursue the matter further or change the subject. Separation and divorce were never easy issues for men to deal with. Ben put his hand on Howie's shoulder to comfort him.

"Hey, pal," he said, "if there's anything we can do, just let us know. We've all had our share of marriage problems, so we sure understand."

"Ain't that the truth," added Tory. "And take it from somebody who's been through it, it may be tough now, but someday you might just realize it was for the best."

Frank shook his head, hoping to get Tory's attention. He knew that was not what Howie needed to hear.

"I don't see how anyone could ever say that losing your wife and kids could ever be for the best," said Howie as he stared at Tory.

The others looked at Tory, hoping he would simply not respond. Unfortunately, that was impossible for him to do. "Hey, look, I'm on your side, Howie. I feel your pain. I've been through it and I feel sorry for you. I'm just trying to make you realize that it's not the end of the world. After the pain goes away and things settle down, I think you'll find the single life is not so bad. You won't have to listen to the Misses complain about all the things you forgot to do; that you stayed out too late with the boys; that you watch too many ball games. Marriage ain't nothing but two people trying to satisfy their own needs anyway. A woman gets married because she wants someone to protect her and take care of her kids. And a man gets married to satisfy certain biological needs, if you know what I mean. How's that old saying, *why buy the cow when the milk's so cheap?*"

The other men looked at Tory in disbelief. They knew he was often stubborn and insensitive, but this was excessive even for him. They wondered how Howie would respond. It did not take long for their curiosity to be satisfied.

"Tory," said Howie as his face reddened, "you're an idiot."

"What?"

"You're an idiot, and I'm a bigger idiot for ever listening to you. You're a bitter, lonely man. You've had not one wife, but three, leave you. You don't know where your children are. You drink too much. You don't eat right. You don't know anything about marriage but how to screw it up, and you still give everybody else advice on what to do about theirs. Well, I've got news for you. I'm not listening to you any more. I love my wife and kids and I'm going to do everything I can to get them back, so I'd appreciate it if you don't remind me any more about how lucky I am that they're gone."

Before Tory or anyone else could respond, Howie quickly rose from the table, picked up his bowling bag, and walked out the door. Within seconds, he was in his truck heading home. He first thought of going to his sister-in-law's house and begging his wife to come home, but soon decided against it. He knew she would not want him appearing so late in the evening. And - even as distraught as he was - he realized he had little chance of being successful and convincing her to come home.

He drove home and parked his truck in the driveway. He slowly climbed down from the truck and walked into his house and withdrew a beer from the refrigerator. He then walked into the living room and threw himself into a chair. If it was possible, he now felt worse than ever. It was not bad enough that his wife and kids had left him, but now everyone at work would soon know about it. And, to make it even worse, he had made a fool of himself in front of his friends. Even though there was no call for what Tory had said, he should not have responded as he did. He should have ignored him as he had done so many times before. He sat drinking his beer, wishing desperately for someone to talk to - someone who could remove the pain and loneliness. At one o'clock the lights went off in Howie Taylor's house.

_____

LuAnn Taylor gradually slowed her car as she neared her house. She wanted to make sure her husband was not at home before she stopped. Since it was a workday, she was almost certain he would not be home, but she didn't want to take a chance. Only after she was certain that his truck was not in sight did she hit the control to open the garage door. Even then she moved slowly, making certain he had not parked his truck in the garage. When she was certain he was not home she parked her car and entered the house. She gasped as she entered the living room.

"Howie!" she exclaimed, "what are you doing here?"

"Well, I thought I still lived here," explained her husband as he entered the room.

"Oh," she said nervously as she stepped backward, "I mean, I didn't see your truck."

"It's parked down the street."

"Why?"

"Because if you had seen it you wouldn't have stopped, and I really need to talk to you."

"Oh," she said, rubbing her hands as he moved toward her.

"Look, Lou," he said, as he walked slowly closer, "you don't have to be afraid. I've never struck you before, have I?"

"No," she answered with a nervous laugh, "but then you've probably never been so angry at me either."

"I'm not angry with you now. I just want to talk to you for a few minutes - okay?"

Something seemed different about him. Although he was correct when he had stated he had never struck her, it had still always been a concern of hers. She always had felt he had the potential to do so. Even so, he now seemed calmer than she could ever remember him. She didn't understand, but she was curious about what he had to say.

"Uh, okay, I can make us a cup of coffee."

"That sounds good."

The two walked into the kitchen, where LuAnn started the coffee maker. They talked about the weather and their kids as they waited for the coffee to brew. LuAnn poured the coffee, then sat at the table across from her husband. She waited nervously for Howie to begin.

"Well, Lou," he said, "I understand."

"You understand? You understand what?"

"What you've been trying to tell me."

"Oh. Well, what is that?"

"Well, first, let me tell you what I did last night. Are you ready for this?"

"I guess. What?"

"Well," he continued after taking a deep breath, "I was so depressed and feeling sorry for myself that I did something that I had not done in many years - actually since I was a child."

She could see the difficulty he was having in continuing, but decided to say nothing. He soon continued. "I said a prayer. Yes, me - stubborn old redneck Howie. I prayed for God to do something to bring you and the kids back to me - to show me the truth in our situation."

"Well?"

"Well, Lou, I've heard people say that prayer changes things, but I never really believed it. But something happened just after I stopped praying. I really think I understood what you have been going through. Every since you left I've been thinking about nothing but me. I've been thinking about how sad and lonely I've been. How sorry I was for myself that you've left me. Last night, for the first time, I felt your pain. I thought of how miserable and unhappy you must have been to have done what you did. I thought of how lonely and depressed and scared you must be right now. I thought of what a good mother you are and how much pain it must have caused you to take the kids away from me. And I know how frightening it must be to think of raising the kids on your own - to go out and find a job after all this time. I guess, basically, Lou, it's like you said - for the first time since I can remember, I was able to put someone else's feelings and needs above my own."

She looked at him cautiously, encouraged about what she had heard, but unsure if she should trust him.

"There's more," he said, interrupting her thoughts.

"Really?" she asked. "Well, I'm listening."

"I figured that if just a little prayer could open my eyes like that, then maybe I should pursue this a little more. So I got out the Bible and began reading everything I could about marriage."

"You're kidding," responded LuAnn. "And how did you even know where to look?"

"It has an index - a concordance, I guess you call it."

"So what did you discover?" she asked, now becoming more interested in what he had to say.

"Well, first I read the part about where man and woman were created. Well..., let me read it to you."

He hurriedly left the room and soon returned with their bible. "Okay," he began as he opened it to pages he had marked earlier, "let me start here. This is Genesis chapter two, verse 21. It says, "And the Lord God caused a deep sleep to fall upon Adam, and he slept: and he took one of his ribs, and closed up the flesh instead thereof; And the rib, which the Lord God had taken from man, made he a woman, and brought her unto the man. And Adam said, 'This is now bone of my bones, and flesh of my flesh; she shall be called Woman, because she was taken out of Man.' Therefore, shall a man leave his father and his mother, and shall cleave unto his wife, and they shall be one flesh."

"That's what they read at our wedding," said LuAnn. "Don't you remember?"

"Yeah, I guess I do," he responded, "but to tell you the truth, Lou, I guess I really never gave it much thought."

"So now that you're thinking about it, what does it mean to you?"

"I guess just what it says. That a man and woman are meant to be together - that nothing should come between them."

"So," she said slowly, "you're pointing out what a terrible thing I did when I left you?"

"Oh, no," he answered quickly, "that's not what I meant. It just shows how important marriage is. Anyway, that's not the important part."

"There's more?"

"Oh, yeah, I did a lot of reading. But there's only one more part I want to read to you. Do you remember when we talked about a man being the head of the family?"

"Oh yes. Are you going to tell me that you found something to support that?"

"Well, sort of," he answered as he continued to flip through the pages. "Just let me find it. Oh, here it is, Ephesians chapter five, verse 21. "Submitting yourselves one to another in the fear of God. Wives, submit yourselves unto your own husbands, as unto the Lord. For the husband is the head of the wife even as Christ is the head of the church: and he is the Savior of the body. Therefore as the church is subjective unto Christ, so let the wives be to their husbands in everything."

He waited for her reaction. It didn't take long.

"You're kidding?" she said. "It really says that?"

He showed to her the verses from which he had just read. She looked at it and shook her head in disbelief.

"Well, I guess you've been right this whole time. But I have to tell you, Howie, it's really hard for me to accept a God that gives laws like that. A man dominating his wife - why, that's almost like slavery."

"That's what I thought at first but...well, don't get too upset until you hear the rest."

"Oh. Okay, go ahead."

He continued to read. "Verse 25 - Husbands, love your wives, even as Christ also loved the Church, and gave himself for it; That he might sanctify and cleanse it with the washing of water by the word, That he might present it to himself a glorious church, not having spot or wrinkle, or any such thing; but that it should be holy and without blemish. So ought men to love their wives as their own bodies. He that loveth his wife loveth himself. For no man ever yet hated his own flesh; but nourishteth and cherisheth it, even as the Lord the church."

She looked at him silently, pondering what he had read. "Well," she said slowly, "that's a lot to think about. What does that mean to you?"

"Well, I guess what it means is that a husband has to love his wife more than he loves himself - that he has to place her needs first in everything. It looks like the first verse is saying that a man even has to sacrifice his life for his wife."

"That's pretty heavy," she said as she took the bible from him and read the passage herself. She finished reading and turned back to him.

"Well, Howie, since you've had more time to think about this than I have, what does this whole thing mean to you? Can you, like, summarize it for me?"

"I'll try. First of all, I think a person has to understand what God means about the man being the head of the family. I noticed that it doesn't say that the man should dominate or boss the woman, but that she should submit herself to the husband."

"I don't see the difference."

"Well, I guess basically, it's directed to the woman to give control to the husband - it's not up to the husband to demand it. And I guess God set it up that way because the man is bigger and stronger."

"Oh, Okay. What about the second part."

"Well, I think because men were created bigger and stronger, they have to protect the wife and family - even to the point of sacrificing themselves. It looks like we're supposed to use Jesus as our example - How He sacrificed Himself for mankind. What do you think about all of this?"

"Wow," she responded after thinking for a few seconds. "Like I said, this is pretty heavy. I'm still in shock a little I guess."

They sat silently for a moment, both sipping their coffee and looking at each other. Finally, Lou spoke again.

"To tell you the truth, Howie, I think this is great. I had no idea the Bible spelled out in this kind of detail what a marriage should be. But there's one thing I have to ask. Do you really believe this? I mean, do you really think you can do this?"

"Well, honey," he answered as he looked into her eyes, "all I can tell you is that I'll try my best. I realize what a fool I've been, and how much I've hurt you and the kids. I also know how much I love you. I don't think I can live without you and Tina and Travis, so I'm willing to do whatever it takes. There's one thing I have to say, though. I honestly believe that, according to what we've just read, the man's role is tougher than the woman's. I mean, I know it would be difficult for you to submit yourself to me as head of the family - especially after everything I've done, but, putting you first in everything - that will be rough."

"I agree," she said with a laugh. "That would be tough for anyone - redneck or not. But I can see," she added seriously, "how it would make a marriage stronger if a couple could do that."

"I agree. And, as I said, I'll try. I'm not going to ask you again, Lou - -it has to be your decision - but I sure miss you and would like you to come home."

"One other thing. Can we start going to church? I think we both need it."

"Okay," he responded.

She arose and moved toward him, seating herself in his lap. He wrapped his arms around her waist as she pressed his head against her breast.

"Howie," she said softly, "I just want you to know that I think this is the most loved I've ever felt. Thank you for doing what you did."

He took her face in his hands and gently kissed her lips. "Welcome home," he whispered.

SEVENTY TIMES SEVEN

AUGUST, 1989

It was a beautiful summer evening in San Jose. The temperature was in the low eighties, and a gentle breeze drifted down from San Francisco Bay. A few clouds floated overhead, occasionally blocking the warm, evening sun. Children's laughter filled the street of the working class neighborhood where the Tanaka family lived. Julie Tanaka sat on the steps in front of the house she shared with her older brother and his family. She read a romance novel as her nephew rode his tricycle along the sidewalk. She often imagined herself as the heroine in the stories, fantasizing of the many wonderful places described - New York, Las Vegas, or perhaps Acapulco. Someday her life would be as exciting as the women in the stories, but not today.

She realized, at nineteen, that her life was only beginning. And she also realized that she had much for which to be thankful. Mostly, she was thankful for her older brother, Johnny, for opening his house to her when their mother had died three years earlier. She got along well with her sister-in-law Tricia, and she adored her three-year-old nephew, Rickey. For that reason she did not mind watching him during the day while her brother and his wife worked. She also enjoyed her part-time job as a waitress, as well as the classes she took two evenings a week.

But still, she felt that she should be doing more with her life. And she hated that she had to rely on her brother for support. Although he was responsible and stable, he could be a very difficult person with which to live. She felt that he took life too seriously. He, in turn, felt that she was irresponsible - even, at times, a scatterbrain. This was the thing that bothered her most - to be supported by a brother who showed such little respect for her.

She put down her book and ran to her nephew who had wandered too near the street. She was directing him back toward the house when her brother and sister-in-law emerged from the side door.

"We're leaving now, Julie," said her brother as he and his wife walked to their son and gave him a hug.

"Where are you going?" asked Rickey.

"We're going to meet some people for dinner, honey," responded his mother. "You'll be staying here with Aunt Julie."

"Can I go, Mommy?" he asked. "I like eating with people, too."

"I know, honey," she smiled, "but these are friends of Daddy's from work. It's not a dinner for little kids. But you and Aunt Julie will have a good time at home."

"Okay," he returned as he smiled at his aunt.

"Now, Julie," said her brother, "remember, he's to be in bed by eight-thirty, and…"

"I do this all the time, Johnny, remember? I'm the one who watches him during the day."

"Okay," he said. "Just be careful."

They hugged their son before getting in the car and driving away. Rickey waived until they were out of sight.

Julie soon returned to her story, frequently glancing at her nephew as he continued to play in the driveway. He had scattered his toys in the driveway and was maneuvering around them with his tricycle. A smile came to her lips as she watched him. She wondered if his parents knew how lucky they were to have such a wonderful child.

An idea came to her as she watched her nephew playing. "Hey, Rickey," she called, "it's time for dinner. How would you like to go down to Waldo's for a hamburger?"

"Can I get a milkshake, too?" he asked.

"You can have anything you like."

"Okay," he responded. "But I have to put my toys away so daddy won't be mad."

She went to Rickey and began helping him pick up his toys. She knew that Johnny would be angry if he learned that they had gone out without asking first, but he'd get over it. Besides, it was only a few blocks to the neighborhood hangout. And, if she were lucky, Tony Tayama would be there.

They cleared the driveway of the toys and locked the doors to the house. They climbed into her ancient Chrysler LeBaron, which was parked on the street. The car was not attractive to look at, but it was still mechanically sound. Julie put Rickey in his car seat and fastened the belt, then jumped into the driver's seat. She looked both ways, then eased the car away from the curb.

Rickey talked aimlessly about all the things he might order for dinner as they drove to the restaurant. Julie made sure she observed the thirty MPH speed limit. She knew the local police patrolled the neighborhood, hoping to catch someone going even five miles over the speed limit.

From nowhere, a football came bouncing in front of her car, causing Julie to swerve the car to the left. At the same instant, two teenagers in the parked car across the street - oblivious to her situation - roared into the street in her direction. Upon seeing the oncoming car, Julie jerked the car back into her lane. As she did so, her foot reached for the brake, but, in her panic, hit the accelerator instead. She found the brake just as the car jumped the sidewalk. Hitting the brake on the grass made the car slide sideways. The last thing she remembered was the sound of crunching metal as the car hit the tree.

Julie didn't know how long she'd been unconscious. The first thing she heard was a man's voice saying, "Let's get him into the wagon".

She raised her head from the stretcher and looked around to see a number of people nearby, staring down at her. It was not until she saw the crumpled car that she remembered what had happened. When she did so, she began screaming, "Rickey, Rickey. Where's Rickey?"

Within seconds a young man in a uniform was at her side. "Now, calm down, Miss Tanaka," he said taking her hand. "Everything is going to be fine."

"Is he all right?" she demanded.

"You'll both be fine," he assured her. "You both just have a few cuts and bruises, but you'll both be fine."

"Are you sure?" she pleaded.

"Trust me," he continued. "Like I said, your nephew has a few cuts but he will be fine. As a matter of fact, while we were putting him in the wagon he wanted to know if he could get a milkshake at the hospital."

His words brought a smile to her face. Even so, the pain in her heart was much worse than the pain in her body. How could she have allowed such a thing to happen? Perhaps her brother was right - she was a scatterbrain. Although she was relieved that her nephew was going to be okay, she didn't think she could ever face her brother again. She lay back and closed her eyes, hoping, that when she opened them, it would be a bad dream.

JUNE, 2002

Johnny Tanaka had hoped that, by ten o'clock, the traffic would have died down. Unfortunately, that was not the case. Although he could see the San Francisco skyline drawing nearer, he realized they would not be on time for their appointment. He was irritated with himself for not insisting that he pick his son up sooner. And he was irritated with his ex-wife for insisting that Rickey finish his music lesson before leaving. His son could feel his displeasure.

"Dad," he said, "I don't see why we don't just forget this and go home. It's not going to do any good anyway."

"Rickey," answered his father, "we'll only be about ten minutes late. Besides, no doctor is ever on time. We'll be there before he's even ready for us."

"You know it's not going to do any good. I don't know why you keep taking me to these doctors."

"Someday you'll thank me for this," answered Johnny. "This doctor is from Johns Hopkins University. He's one of the leading doctors in the country in neuromuscular injuries and rehabilitation."

"Well that's great, Dad, but I've already told you, I'm happy with the way I am now. I don't see why you can't accept it."

"Accept you being a cripple for the rest of your life? I'll never accept it and I don't see how you can either, Rickey."

"I'm not a cripple, Dad. I have a limp. I don't know why we're even having this conversation. We've been through this a dozen times. You're not going to be happy until this doctor tells you there's nothing he can do."

"I'm only doing this for you, son," he answered. "Someday I hope you'll see that."

The two continued their drive in silence. Ten minutes later, they turned into an office building and parked the car and quickly found Doctor Dyson's office. As Johnny Tanaka had expected, the receptionist informed him that the doctor would be with them soon. Soon, the nurse came out and led Rickey into the doctor's office. She told Johnny that, after the examination, he would talk to the two together.

Johnny waited anxiously to be called. It was thirty minutes before he was allowed to join his son in the doctor's office.

"Mr. Tanaka," said the doctor as he arose from his desk, "I'm Doctor Dyson."

"Glad to meet you, Doctor," said Johnny. "I've heard great things about you."

The two chatted for a moment before the conversation centered on Rickey.

"Well, Mr. Tanaka," said the doctor, "I've examined Rickey and - well, first, let me ask you a question. I've talked to Rickey and I think I know where he's coming from, but I would like to know what you expect?"

"Well, I don't think it's realistic to expect that he'll ever be 100% normal, but I'd like to see as much improvement as possible."

"What kind of improvement?"

"To be able to walk without a limp. To be able to do things that other kids his age do. You know - run, jump, play sports."

"Mr. Tanaka," said Doctor Dyson, "You've probably heard this before, but considering the accident your son had, he's really quite lucky."

"What you're getting at is that you can do nothing for him?"

"Mr. Tanaka," he continued. "In the car wreck, your son experienced a great deal of damage to the muscles and nerves in his leg. He tells me that he's had many years of therapy to strengthen the leg, and I would say that it might be beneficial to continue that from time to time, but I don't think we can expect much more improvement."

"I've heard that you are one of the best doctors in your field. And now…."

"Thank you. I like to think I have a little skill, but I'm still only a doctor - not God. And if you don't mind me making an observation, I think Rickey has accepted his situation quite well. Rickey, what interests you in life? Do you want to be an athlete?"

"No, not really," answered Rickey. "I enjoy music and photography. I've tried to tell my dad that, but he won't listen."

Johnny Tanaka felt embarrassment at his son's remark. How

could he make him realize that he only wanted the best for him? Doctor Dyson recognized his pain.

"Look, Mr. Tanaka," he said, "we all want to protect our children. I understand what you're trying to do, but sometimes you just have to let it go. As I said, Rickey has accepted his situation. Now I think it's time for you to do the same."

The meeting ended soon. Although Johnny was not pleased with the doctor's opinion, he thanked him for his time as they left the room. Doctor Dyson watched in silence as Rickey picked up his cane and limped out of his office.

The two rode home in silence. By lunchtime they were again back in San Jose. As they pulled up in front of Rickey's house, he turned to his father.

"Dad," he began, "I do appreciate what you're trying to do, but it's like the doctor said - we just have to accept it. There's nothing else we can do."

His father smiled and nodded his head. Before leaving, Rickey turned back to his father.

"Dad, there's one more thing. I really believe you should go to Aunt Julie's wedding. I think…"

"Rickey, I really don't wish to discuss this again."

Rickey knew that it was useless to pursue the subject. He said goodbye to his father and walked slowly into his house.

Johnny Tanaka arose early the next morning. Being self-employed as a graphic artist it was not necessary to arise so early, but it was a custom he had inherited from his parents and continued to observe. By eight o'clock he had completed his exercises, showered, and eaten breakfast. He seated himself at his computer to begin working on his latest project - designing a brochure for a medical equipment manufacturer. He felt lucky to have a job that was both enjoyable and so financially rewarding. The fact that he could perform his work at home was an added bonus. He had only begun his work when the phone rang.

"Hi, Johnny," came the familiar response at the other end.

"Hey, Lori. It's good to hear from you, but I didn't expect you to call until this afternoon. Is everything all right?"

"Oh, yeah," replied Lori Yakama. "Our meeting doesn't start for a few more minutes so I just thought I'd call."

"How has your trip been?"

"Oh, it's fine, but you know how I hate to travel. I'll be glad to get home."

"We still on for dinner tonight?"

"Sure. I'll call you when I get in. How was the meeting with the doctor yesterday?"

"About the same as all the others. I wasn't too impressed with him."

"Oh, I'm sorry. I guess we can talk about it tonight."

"Yeah. You sure you don't want me to pick you up at the airport?"

"Oh, no, that's fine. Three of us are sharing a cab so it'll be no problem. What time do you want me over?"

"Around seven - or whenever you get here. It'll be good to see you."

"Me too," she answered. "Got to run. I'll see you tonight."

Johnny put the phone down and returned to his work. Even though Lori had only been gone four days, he had really missed her. This was the first time in their six-month relationship that he'd gone so long without seeing her. Perhaps tonight would be the time to discuss where their relationship was going.

As he reached for a notebook on his desk, his eyes were drawn to a familiar pink envelope. He picked it up and examined the card inside as he had done many times before. The front of the invitation read:

WE ASK YOU TO SHARE IN OUR JOY
AS GOD JOINS
Julie Tanaka & Roger Toya
IN HOLY MATRIMONY

He stared at the announcement for a moment before tossing it aside. He knew his sister would be very hurt if he were not there. For a second, he felt compassion for her. For a second, he felt her pain. Then, in a moment, it was swept away. Let her be hurt. Perhaps now she would realize the pain she had caused him, and his son, thirteen years earlier. Perhaps only now - when her only brother refused to attend her wedding - would she truly realize what it was like to suffer.

———————

As usual, Lori was right on time. Johnny kissed her warmly before inviting her into his house. He handed her a glass of wine. The two seated themselves on the couch and discussed the past few days' events. Lori told him about her conference in San Diego. He then informed her about the visit to the doctor. Although she stated that she was sorry, he realized that she, like his son, had expected nothing to come from the visit. Since he did not wish to discuss the matter again, he soon changed the subject.

He soon excused himself to light the barbecue grill. When it was hot enough, he put on the steaks. The two enjoyed a leisurely meal on the patio, sipping their wine and chatting as they ate. Once finished, they returned to the living room and continued their conversation. Soon, Lori turned to Johnny with a more serious look.

"Johnny," she said, "I've had a lot of time to think about things the last few days and - well, there's something that's bothering me."

"Yes?" he answered slowly.

"Well, I know you don't want to discuss this, but I need to. I really think you should go to your sister's wedding. I think this is a good time to make amends with her."

He set down his glass of wine and shook his head.

"I'm not sure I understand this. You don't even know my sister. Why is this a concern of yours? Has Rickey said something to you?"

"No," she answered quickly, "absolutely not. If you must know why it concerns me I'll tell you. I really don't understand how you can go for over ten years without speaking to your only sister because of something that was an accident."

"It was more than just an accident. She knew she was not to take Rickey anywhere in the car. We had discussed it before. Basically she was putting her own selfishness - her own desire to meet one of her boyfriends - over my son's safety. And her selfishness caused him to be a cripple for the rest of his life. I still don't understand why you have more concern for someone you've never met than you do for me."

"It's more than that, Johnny," she answered after taking a deep breath. "You don't seem to forget or forgive anything, and that really bothers me. What happens if I do something to upset you? Do you just write me off, too?"

"That's ridiculous," he answered. "It hasn't happened yet, has it? And what do you mean by saying I never forget or forgive anything? I don't think that's a fair statement. Give me an example."

"I shouldn't have said that," she answered. "I'm sorry."

"No, if you said that then you must have had a reason. I would like to know what it is. What other things have I been unable to forget?"

"Okay, how about your marriage? You never want to discuss it with me but I know you only talk to Trish when it's absolutely necessary. And if it wasn't necessary for Rickey's sake, you would never speak to her."

"I don't believe this," he said as he stood and put his hands on his hips. "You don't even know what it's like to go through a divorce. How many people do you know that have been through a divorce who are still friends? Is that your only example?"

"No," she answered, "it's not. I might as well get it all in the open. It also bothers me when you talk about what happened to your parents. You still blame the government for their deaths."

"Dammit!" he said bitterly, "they were responsible. The internment camp killed my parents. You're Japanese, too, aren't you? You know how many of our parents and grandparents were put in those camps during the war."

"But your father lived many years after they were released, and your mother only died fifteen years ago. How can you say it killed them? That's been over fifty years ago."

"Neither one of them were the same after that. Despite what you say, I know that the camp killed them. It may have taken some time but it killed them."

"I don't know," she said wearily, "maybe you're right. But that's not really the point. The point is that you are still bitter about something that happened so long ago. That's what really bothers me."

"Well," he said more calmly, "I'm sorry if I'm not perfect, Lori, but I think I have a right to be upset over the things we talked about. All I can ask you is to try and accept me with my faults."

"And if I can't?" she asked with a crack in her voice.

"Then I don't know what to tell you," he replied.

She turned to him with a tear in her eyes. She sat silent for a few seconds, then placed her glass on the table, and arose from the couch.

"Well then," she said with a crack in her voice, "I guess I know what I have to do."

She picked up her purse and turned toward the door, waiting for him to stop her, to apologize and ask her to stay. He said nothing. She stopped at the door and turned back to him.

"Goodbye, Johnny," she said softly, and then she was gone.

Johnny sat silently for a few minutes, staring blankly out the window. He then suddenly arose, threw his glass against the wall, and rushed out the door. His first thought was to go immediately to Lori's apartment and beg her to come back - to convince her that everything would be all right - that he would change. But then he realized he could not do that. She had walked out on him - let her make the first move. He would wait for her to come to her senses.

He started the car and drove aimlessly around the town. He soon came to a small bar that he had heard of. It was not one that he and Lori had visited, so there would be no one there to ask questions. He parked his Trans Am and walked inside.

It was early, so the place was only sparsely filled. He seated himself on a bar stool and ordered a beer. Sitting silently, he sipped his drink and thought of everything that had happened recently. His son had as much as told him that he didn't need his assistance anymore. As tactful as the doctor had tried to be, he knew what he was really saying - grow up and accept life as it is - quit trying to change things that can't be changed. And now Lori, the woman he loved, had told him she couldn't live with his pride - his stubbornness. Never had he felt so alone.

He occasionally spoke to the bartender as he drank his beer. He soon ordered another, nursing it as he pondered his life. Eventually realizing that the alcohol would do nothing to solve his problems, he finished his last sip of beer he returned to his car.

A light rain began falling as he climbed into his car and headed home. Although he was only a few miles from his house, it was not a neighborhood with which he was familiar. He drove slowly for a while, searching for a familiar street which would lead him home. As his patience increased, so did his speed.

If it had not been raining - or if the overgrown bush had not partially blocked his view - perhaps he would have seen the stop sign in time. As it happened, by the time he saw it, it was too late. He went through the intersection at thirty-five miles per hour. He didn't see the car until it was only a few feet away - and only a split second before he heard the sound of metal crunching against metal. It was a sickening sound - one he would never forget.

His first thought was how lucky he was that he always used his seatbelt. Despite the strength of the impact, he didn't seem to be hurt. He removed his seatbelt, opened the door and exited the car, and immediately collapsed on the ground.

―――――――――

The next thing Johnny saw was someone dressed in white standing a few feet away. The surroundings were unfamiliar to him. It took a moment to realize that he was in a hospital room.

"Excuse me," he said as he raised his arm.

"Yes," answered the nurse.

"What - how - uhh-" he began.

"You were brought in last night after the accident," she answered.

"Am I - will I - " he stammered as he tried to gain control of his thoughts.

"You'll be fine," she returned flatly. "You just have a concussion."

"Oh," he said with a sigh, as the memories of last night slowly started to return.

"What about the other driver?" he asked.

"The young lady is not so lucky," answered the nurse, in a tone that led him to believe that was the particular question for which she had been waiting. "At the present, she has no movement or feeling from her waist down."

"Oh, no," he said as he fell back on the pillow. "Oh, God, no. I don't even know what happened."

"Most drunks don't," she replied as she turned and left the room.

He lay in silence, trying to piece together what had happened. Had he really been drunk? He had had only two beers - and the glass of wine at his house earlier. Maybe this was a bad dream and he would wake up soon.

His thoughts were interrupted by someone entering his room.

He looked up to see a uniformed policeman walking toward his bed. His heart began to pound wildly.

"Mr. Tanaka," the officer said, "I'm Officer Daugherty."

"Yes?"

"Well," continued the officer, "I guess this is your lucky day. We just got the results of your blood test. Your alcohol level was below the line for DUI. Right now the only thing we're charging you with is running a stop sign. Depending on what we find, there may be other charges later."

The images of the night before suddenly came back to him.

"There was a bush covering the stop sign," he blurted out.

"I examined the crash site, and, while there was a bush nearby, the sign was still visible. But you'll get the chance to bring that up in court."

With that statement, he removed his citation book and began writing a ticket. When finished he handed it to Johnny to sign. When he had done so, he handed him a copy and turned to walk away. Johnny called after him.

"Officer, what about the girl?"

"If you're asking how she is, all I know is that she has no use of her legs. If you're asking if she plans on filing a civil suit against you, I guess you'll have to take that up with her."

He turned and walked out of the room. Johnny lie back on the bed, staring at the ceiling. With the affect of whatever medication they had given him, he was soon asleep.

It was a couple of hours later that his sleep was interrupted by someone calling his name. He awoke to see a gray-haired man sitting beside his bed.

"Mr. Tanaka," he began, "I'm Dr. Hernandez. How are you feeling?"

"I've had better days, Doctor." he answered. "Maybe you can tell me how I'm doing."

"Well," he responded, "medically speaking I'd say you're doing fine. You had a concussion, but the CAT scan didn't show any signs of internal bleeding. And you will probably be pretty sore for a few days. We'll just have to wait and see if there was any whiplash, but basically, you're fine. I would just like to keep you here until this afternoon and then you can go home. Do you have someone that can pick you up?"

He thought for a moment before answering.

"No, I'll just take a taxi."

"Well then, if you have some questions I'll be around."

He arose from his chair to leave. Johnny leaned forward on one elbow.

"Doctor," he began, "how is the girl? Do you think she'll be all right?"

"Well, to be honest, it doesn't look too good. Along with a few other less-serious injuries, Ms. Kinney has a cracked vertebra in her back. There's been no intrusion into the spinal canal, but there's been a lot of trauma and swelling in the area. All we can do right now is wait and see if there has been any permanent damage to the spinal cord."

"Oh," said Johnny as his eyes began to burn. The doctor turned and left the room.

He was left to himself for the rest of the morning. Occasionally, a nurse would walk in to take his pulse and temperature, but no other visitors came. He thought of calling his son or his ex-wife, or perhaps even Lori, but decided against it. He needed more time to think. Besides, he would be leaving in the afternoon so he could contact them then.

A short time later the nurse delivered his lunch. It was the same one whom had commented about him being a drunk. He tried to start a conversation with her - to show her he was not the type of person she believed him to be. After a few words, however, he realized it was useless, and ate his lunch in silence.

Dr. Hernendez returned in the afternoon to examine him once more. After doing so, he informed him that he was released to go home. Before leaving, he made a statement which caught him off guard. "Oh, Mr. Tanaka," he said, "I've been asked to tell you that Ms. Kinney would like to see you before you leave."

"Ms. Kinney?"

"Yes, you know. The young lady that you - that you were in the accident with."

"And she wants to talk to me? About what?"

"I don't know. I guess you'll have to wait and ask her. She's in room 317."

He patted him on the shoulder, turned and walked out of the room. Johnny lie quietly for a moment, pondering what the woman wanted. Did she plan on saying how much she hated him? Did she wish to increase his guilt by forcing him to see her in her present condition? Or did she simply need to see the man whom had ruined her life? He thought briefly about ignoring her request and quietly leaving the hospital, but he soon dismissed that idea. Knowing that he would have to face her sooner or later, he decided he might as well get it over with. He slowly got dressed and began the long journey to her room.

He entered her room cautiously. He slowly walked behind the curtain, which separated her bed from the adjoining one, currently unoccupied. As he moved from behind the curtain, the young woman came into view. He expected to see someone hooked up to various machines and tubes. Instead, he saw an attractive young Black woman talking and smiling with an older woman seated nearby. The girl appeared to be in her early twenties. He guessed the other woman to be her mother. As he drew nearer, the women noticed him. Before he could speak the older woman arose from her chair, kissed her daughter on the cheek, and turned to walk away. She said nothing to Johnny but smiled sadly as she walked by.

"Mr. Tanaka?" the young girl asked.

"Yes," he responded faintly, "I - I'm Johnny Tanaka."

"I'm Beverly Kinney. Won't you sit down?"

"Okay," he returned, wondering how she could be so pleasant. She extended her hand. He took it and gave a slight shake.

"Ms. Kinney," he continued as he sat down, "I want you to know how sorry I am. I would give anything if this had never happened."

"So would I," she responded as she wiped a tear from her eye. "But there's nothing we can do to change it now."

"Ms. Kinney, there's something else I need to make clear. You've probably heard that I was drinking. Well, I only had two beers. I'm not an alcoholic - in fact I drink very little. The officer will tell you that I was not drunk. As you know, it was very rainy last night. And the stop sign was almost hidden by a bush. And I wasn't familiar with the neighborhood. I just..."

"It's okay, Mr. Tanaka," she interrupted, "I know it was an accident. I forgive you."

"You what?" he asked quickly.

"I said I forgive you."

He stared at her for a few seconds, pondering what she had said. He was both happy and confused. Happy because her remark led him to believe that there would be no civil charges - no long, drawn-out court proceedings. But he was confused about how someone could have just gone through what she had and still find it in her heart to forgive the person that had perhaps destroyed her life. He felt a lump in his throat.

"Ms. Kinney," he said, "I want you to know I'm very grateful for you saying that, but I don't understand how - I mean do you ... "

"Mr. Tanaka," she answered, "I'm not super-human. As a matter of fact, I think I'm still in shock about this right now. But it's only going to make matters worse for both of us if I hate you and try to get revenge. I want to try to get on with my life and the best way to do that is to forgive you."

He looked at her, trying to think of the right words to say. None came.

"Mr. Tanaka," she continued, "I appreciate your coming, but right now I'm really tired. I think I need to sleep for a while."

He nodded his understanding as he arose.

"Ms. Kinney," he said, "again I'm so sorry. If there's anything I can do, please let me know."

She forced a smile as she raised her hand. He reached out his hand to hers then, to his own amazement, he bent forward and kissed it, then turned and walked away.

As he reached the door he was met by an older man entering the room. He guessed him to be Ms. Kinney's grandfather. The two nodded to each other politely and passed by.

Johnny Tanaka was shaken by his encounter with Beverly Kinney. He needed a few moments to think - to calm his nerves - before beginning home. He took the elevator to the basement where he visited the cafeteria and chose a cup of coffee. Taking a seat in the corner of the room, he sat silently, looking out the window and pondering his life.

———————————

Having taken a sleeping pill the night before, Johnny did not awake until after nine the next morning. He had not told anyone about his experience of the last 24 hours, and still did not know if he ever would. In fact, he'd not spoken to anyone since the incident. In reality, he had few people with whom he could discuss something so personal. His son, Lori, and perhaps, his ex-wife. And currently, he was not on the best of terms with any of them. Since his talk with Beverly Kinney, he had spent much time evaluating his life. He felt that something must change, but he still was not sure what.

He had just poured himself a cup of coffee when the doorbell rang. He wondered who it could be so early in the morning. "Probably just another salesman", he thought to himself. He sat down his coffee and walked to the door.

When he saw his visitor, he was both surprised and confused. It was a few seconds before he recognized the man, but it slowly came back to him. It was the older gentleman he had seen entering Ms. Kinney's room the previous day.

"Mr. Tanaka," said his visitor, "I'm Frederick Kinney. We almost met yesterday in my granddaughter's hospital room."

"Yes, I remember," Johnny replied as he absentmindedly held out his hand.

"May I come in?" asked Mr. Kinney as he shook his hand.

"Oh, sure," Johnny replied after a few seconds delay. "Can I get you a cup of coffee?"

"That would be fine, thank you."

With shaking hands Johnny poured a cup of coffee as Mr. Kinney stood nearby. After handing him the coffee he again began to explain how terrible he felt about the accident.

"I understand how you feel, Mr. Tanaka. I spoke to Beverly for quite some time yesterday, but I really didn't come here to discuss my Granddaughter."

"No?" answered Johnny.

"May we sit down?"

"Oh yes, please do."

The two men walked to the family room. His visitor seated himself in a chair while Johnny chose the nearby couch facing him.

"Mr. Tanaka," he continued. "I plan on being very blunt here. I guess when you get older you just say what you think. I'm also a minister so there's not much I haven't seen in my life. I told you I didn't come here to discuss my granddaughter. I came here to discuss you."

"Me? I don't understand."

"Yesterday, when I got to Beverly's room, she asked me to go get her something to drink. So I went down to the cafeteria. I saw you sitting there, staring out the window. God spoke to me, Mr. Tanaka. He said you are a deeply troubled man - a man with a lot of bitterness in your heart. I went back up and talked to Beverly. She told me about your conversation. From what she said, you didn't have any concept of how she could forgive you."

"Well, yeah, I think I do. She said it would be better for her so she could get along with her life. That makes sense to me. I think

I understand."

"I really don't think you do," he returned bluntly. "First, I want to tell you a story. I think it will help me make my point."

"Okay," said Johnny, feeling as if he had no choice in the matter.

"I'm not from California. I grew up in the thirties and forties in Mississippi. I'm sure you've heard stories of poor Black families growing up in the Deep South, and how rough they had it, but I don't think anyone can really understand unless they've lived it. Well, our family was actually better off than most. We had our own farm and enough money to get by. I was a pretty lucky kid. I hadn't seen a lot of the hatred and violence a lot of other Black children had experienced. All of that changed when I was thirteen."

"I was walking home from school when my life fell apart. I found my grandfather hanging from a tree. It seems that a bunch of White men decided to make an example of him. Earlier that week a young White woman's car had broken down beside the road. My grandfather's sin was that he gave her a ride home on his horse. I guess he would've been all right if he'd gotten off and walked, but she rode on the back of the horse with him. I guess some folks decided he wasn't good enough to ride on a horse with a White woman."

"I'm sorry," said Johnny softly.

"Well, you can imagine what that did to me. I was filled with more hate and revenge than you can imagine. I swore that I would get even with all White people. And, when I was old enough, I was true to my word. I won't go into any details, but, whenever possible I made White people pay for what they'd done to my grandfather. But you know what? It didn't take away the pain like I thought it would. As a matter of fact, it only made me more bitter and more angry. I was still angry with white people, and now I was angry with myself for the things I had done."

"And then, an amazing thing happened. One night, as I was walking down the road, I heard the most beautiful singing. It was coming from a nearby church. I decided to go in and see what was going on. Well, believe it or not, the preacher's message was on forgiveness. He talked about how Jesus, just before He died on the cross, asked God to forgive His accusers. Well, that night, I accepted Jesus and my whole life changed."

Johnny had been listening to his story, almost in a trance. He understood Mr. Kinney's words when he spoke of anger and revenge. While he hated to admit it, they were feelings he had dealt with most of his life.

"I would like to read a couple of things to you, if I may."

He was surprised that his visitor had asked. But now, he seemed kinder, more compassionate. Mr. Kinney removed a small Bible from his coat pocket.

"Sure," he responded.

"Matthew 18, verse 21 - Then came Peter to Him and said, Lord, how oft shall my brother sin against me and I forgive him? Till seven times? Jesus saith unto him, I say not unto thee, until seven times, but until seventy times seven."

He flipped through the pages quickly.

"And here. Romans 12, verse 19 - Avenge not yourselves but rather give place unto wrath: for it is written, vengeance is mine; I will repay saith the Lord. Be not overcome of evil, but overcome evil with good.

"One more," he explained as he continued. "Ephesians 4, verse 32. Be ye kind one to another, tenderhearted, forgiving one another, even as God, for Christ's sake, hath forgiven you."

He closed the book and waited silently for Johnny to say something. When he got no response, he spoke again.

"Well, was I right in coming here or did I misread God's message?"

Johnny broke into tears. He told him about his parents being sent to the concentration camp only because they were Japanese. He told him of his sister's accident, which crippled his son. He told him of all the terrible things that had happened in his life, which he could never forgive. Finally, after a few minutes, he regained his composure.

"I guess I realize I have a problem. But it's not that easy to change. All those things you read make sense, but I don't think I can just become that kind of person overnight."

"Well, maybe I can put this on a more personal level. God doesn't just tell us things because He wants to make life more difficult for us. He tells us things for our own good. He tells us to forgive one another for a reason. If you don't forgive someone it will actually cause physical problems - high blood pressure, digestive problems, and so on. It will also lead to depression, sleeplessness, and - as you've seen - anger and bitterness. As I discovered, hate makes a person a slave. That's why my granddaughter forgave you - it was as much for herself as it was for you. You see, God just doesn't give us the right to forgive someone, He demands it."

"I, uh, I think I understand," returned Johnny. "But I'm still not sure where to begin."

"Then can I ask you a question?"

"Sure."

"Do you believe in Jesus?"

"I guess I believe in Him. I've never given it much thought."

"You can't believe in Him like you believe there was a President Lincoln. You have to believe that He is the Son of God. You have to ask Him to come into your life."

"How do I do that?"

"You just ask Him. Will you pray with me?"

"Okay."

The two men lowered their heads in prayer. When they had finished, Frederick Kinney left for the hospital to comfort his granddaughter.

Julie Tanaka tried on her wedding dress for the fifth time since she had picked it up. Her wedding was only a few days away. She was both elated and nervous. Luckily, there were many things left to be done so she had little time to worry about the event that would change her life. She removed the dress, put it back on the hangar, and returned it to the closet. As she turned to exit, she brushed against the storage shelf. A book fell at her feet. As she bent to pick it up, she realized it was an old family picture album. The album fell open to display pictures of her family taken years earlier. She saw pictures of her and her brother as youngsters playing at the beach. Tears filled her eyes as she placed the album back on the shelf.

She decided she would call her best friend to discuss her wedding for the tenth time. As she walked into the living room there came a knock at the door. She walked hurriedly to the door and opened it. She gasped when she saw her brother standing there. She tried to speak but could not find the words. She waited for him to explain. Finally, in a low whisper, he said,

"Julie, I'm sorry."

She wanted to hate him for all he had done - for all the many years he'd spent hating her, trying to make her pay for the mistake she'd made - but she could not. Joy overcame her as she moved forward. Tears fell from their eyes as they embraced. It felt good to have her brother back.

The sound of an unanswered phone could be heard coming from Johnny Tanaka's house. After the fourth ring, the answering machine took the call. The caller knew it would be news he would be eager to receive.

"Mr. Tanaka, this is Frederick Kinney. I just thought you would like to know that my granddaughter was able to move her toes this morning. It'll still be a long process, but the doctors think she will be all right. Good day and God Bless."

NOT BY WORKS

Sarah Horton hoped that the bus would be on time. It had been a long and tiring day at work, and the sweltering heat drained what energy she had remaining. She found a seat at the bus stop, and a nearby tree offered shelter from the sun. As she sat waiting for the bus, she found herself wishing she had not volunteered to work at the senior citizen's center. Unfortunately, she never seemed to be able to refuse when the social worker called. But, as tired as she was, it always made her feel good to do something for others. Volunteering also had another benefit. The more time she spent helping others, the less time she spent listening to her mother's criticism. By the time she returned home it would almost be bedtime - possibly only long enough for three or four of her mother's cutting remarks.

She waited a few minutes before the Knoxville city bus arrived. Sarah wearily pulled herself to her feet and climbed the steps, then dropped the change into the coin box. She looked around for a second, then threw herself into the closest seat.

The trip to the senior citizen's center took only twenty minutes. The center was an apartment building which the city had converted to house the elderly. The building was many decades old, but had been well maintained and was still in sound condition. With a supplement from the city, the residents' rent was based on their income. Some paid as much as they would at any similar building, while others paid very little. The city provided a number of activities for the residents in the building's community room. The first floor of the building also housed a number of small businesses, including a convenience store, a dry cleaner, and - probably most important - a pharmacy. As many times as Sarah had been to the building, it almost felt like home. She decided that there were many worse places a person could spend the last few years of their lives.

But the best thing about the building, she decided, was the excellent management the city provided. At least one person was on duty at all times to provide security and assistance to the residents when necessary. Through her many visits, she had become acquainted with one of the managers. Fred Meade, as well as being the evening manager, was the only non-senior citizen resident in the building. A "young whippersnapper", as many of the residents called him. In reality, Sarah estimated him to be between forty-five and fifty, only a few years older than her at forty-two. From their few brief conversations she had learned much about him. She knew that he had worked for twenty-five years for the Tennessee Valley Authority before taking an early retirement. She knew that he had been a widower for almost ten years. And she knew that he had only one child, a daughter, who lived in Florida. She also knew, or at least suspected, that he was attracted to her. He had never asked her for a date - he seemed much too shy - but he always seemed happy to see her and always asked about her job as a librarian. He seemed nice enough - and was a handsome man - but she hoped he would not ask her out. She would hate to turn him down, but she needed no more complications in her life.

Fred Meade peered out over the reception counter as Sarah entered the lobby. As usual, he greeted her warmly.

"Well, good evening, Miss Horton," he said. "You look a little tired. Rough day?"

"Hi, Fred," she answered. "Yes it was. One lady didn't come in so I volunteered to work through lunch. I didn't get a chance to rest all day."

"And you still came here to help out today. You sure have a good heart."

"Well," she replied, "hopefully someday I'll get my reward."

"I'm sure you will."

She set her bag on the counter and removed a piece of paper. She read the name the social worker had given her.

"Mrs. Philpot - I'm supposed to be visiting her tonight. Can you tell me what apartment she's in?"

"Oh, yes," he returned emphatically, "Bertie Philpot. Apartment 318."

"Why do you say it like that? Is she trouble?"

"Oh, no. She's a real sweetie. A little peculiar - maybe a little - I don't know - shall we say spiritual at times. She broke her foot you know."

"Yes, that's why I'm here. I said I would fix her dinner and clean up a bit. I probably won't be here too long."

"Don't bet on it," he said, "she's a talker."

"Thank you," she said as she turned to walk away. Fred looked as if he wanted to speak but, since he said nothing, she entered the elevator and pushed the button for the third floor.

She soon arrived at apartment 318 and tapped on the door.

"The door is open. Come on in," came the immediate, but faint, voice.

She opened the door and entered the apartment, peering around the corner from the short foyer. It was a studio apartment - not quite a one-bedroom but larger than an efficiency. The living and dining area were combined into one large L-shaped room. A small kitchen was found off the dining area. The bedroom - or, more accurately, the sleeping area was a large alcove with a pull-out room divider separating it from the rest of the apartment. The best feature of the apartment, however, was the view. As she entered the living area she saw the Tennessee River through the window. In the middle of the room, with her broken foot resting on an ottoman, sat a frail, gray-haired lady.

"Come on in, Missy," she said, as if she were greeting an old friend. "You must be Sarah."

"Yes, and you're Mrs. Philpot?"

"Of course I am, my dear. Come on in and make yourself comfortable. Sit yourself down and rest a minute. It's a scorcher out there, isn't it? I bet you're tired. Would you like some tea or lemonade? Of course you'll have to get it yourself. This blooming cast has put me out of commission for a while."

"Yes, I see," said Sarah, once she had the opportunity to respond. She moved to the couch near Mrs. Philpot and sat down.

"You can call me Bertie. My name is Beatrice but I like Bertie. Never knew why my parents named me Beatrice. My older brother started calling me Bertie when I was only seven. He's gone now you know."

"I'm sorry to hear that," she returned, then, quickly added, "What did you do to your foot, Mrs., uh, Bertie?"

"Oh, it doesn't take much at my age honey - I'm eighty-five, you know. I was going down to the laundry room - it's just down the hall you know. Well I just tripped. It didn't seem bad at first but it kept hurting. One of my friends finally talked me into seeing a Doctor. Said I had a hairline fracture. Told him I didn't even know I had any hair on my foot. Not much of a sense of humor - those doctors - you know. Anyway, it's not too bad now. I just have to wear this blasted cast for another three or four weeks. But it looks like something good came out of it."

"What's that?" asked Sarah.

"You came to visit me, Missy," she answered with a smile.

The two continued chatting for a while. Sarah enjoyed talking to her new acquaintance. Even though she was many years older than her mother - and, from what she had been told by the social worker, not in the best of health - she seemed to have no cares or complaints about life. Perhaps she could discover her secret and share it with her mother.

After a few moments, Sarah took advantage of a lull in the

conversation to ask, "So, Bertie, are you ready for me to fix you something to eat?"

"Only if you promise to join me. A neighbor brought by some meatloaf. I thought you could just warm that up and maybe put a couple of potatoes in the microwave. How does that sound? I'm sure you haven't had a chance to eat."

Sarah started to refuse, but quickly realized, from what she had seen of her host, that it would probably be useless.

"That would be fine," she answered. "And after that you can let me know what else you need to have done."

It only took a few minutes to warm the meatloaf and bake the potatoes. When it was ready, Sarah helped Bertie walk to the small table. After seating her, she sat herself in the opposite chair. She enjoyed the view of the river as she waited for her host to begin. Noticing that Bertie had bowed her head, she did likewise.

"Dear Lord," she began, "thank you for this food you have given us. Let it nourish our bodies. And thank you for my new friend, Sarah, dear Lord. I ask you to look over her and make sure she gets home okay tonight, Lord. And thank you for helping me make it through another day. In Jesus's name we pray. Amen."

Bertie looked up at Sarah and smiled, and then began to eat. The two continued their conversation between bites.

"So you said you're a librarian, huh?" asked Bertie.

"Yes. For over twenty years."

"You like it?"

"It's okay."

"You married?"

"No."

"Ever been?"

"No."

"Why?"

Sarah laughed at her directness. From someone else, the bluntness of the questions might have been offensive, but, coming from her, she didn't mind.

"I don't know," she answered. "I was involved with a couple of different men when I was younger, but things just didn't work out. I'm an only child and my mother has never been well. I guess maybe I was afraid of leaving her alone. Maybe men were afraid of getting too close to me because of that. I don't know. It doesn't matter now anyway."

"What's wrong with your mother?"

"Oh, bad back, arthritis in her knees, headaches. That's about all at present."

"So, if you're not taking care of your mother or working, you're volunteering to help out old folks like me, right?"

"Well, I guess so," answered Sarah.

"No wonder you're not married. Sure doesn't leave much time for yourself, does it?"

"I guess not, but I don't mind."

"Well," said Bertie, "you sure are a good person, Sarah. Too bad you don't have a life of your own, though."

"It's not that bad. Besides, I'm sure God will reward me when I get to heaven."

"Oh Yeah? How will you know when you've done enough?"

"What do you mean?"

"How will you know when you've done enough good deeds to get to heaven? Maybe God grades on a curve."

"Well, I don't know," she answered with a laugh. "I guess God judges a person's entire life. Besides, He knows what's in a person's heart. What do you think?"

"Oh, I don't have the answer to everything," she said. "But it's something you might want to think about."

Sarah felt that there should have been more to the conversation - that it had been a sort of test-but that Bertie wasn't ready to give her the answer yet. Since Bertie let it drop, she did also.

After finishing their dinner - or supper, as Bertie insisted was the proper southern term - Sarah cleaned the table and placed the dishes in the dishwasher. She then asked what chores needed to be done. Although Bertie insisted that nothing else was necessary, Sarah convinced her to allow her to dust and vacuum the apartment. After the cleaning was done, she again seated herself near her new friend. She quickly learned much about her host. She was a native of Knoxville. For forty years, her husband had owned a small appliance store on the east side of town. He had died ten years earlier, leaving her with a small but adequate pension. She had two sons, who were now married and living in other parts of the country, one in Atlanta and the other in Charlotte. Both had requested that she come and live with them, but she had declined. She told them that she and her husband had always been "Tennessee Hillbillies" and would always be so. Besides, she explained, she was too old and feeble to make such a trip.

She also learned, as she had suspected, that Bertie was a devout Christian. But, to Sarah's surprise, Bertie did not question her beliefs. Sarah was relieved, since it would be a question which she would have much difficulty in answering.

It was after eight when Sarah finally arose to leave. Bertie thanked her many times for her visit and assistance. She told her that she hoped she would see her soon. Sarah agreed to visit her the following week. As she headed for the door, Bertie called after her.

"You don't mind some advice from an old lady, do you?"

"Somehow I don't think it would matter if I did," she answered with a smile.

"You're a pretty young woman. Do something for yourself for a change. You deserve some happiness. And think about what I asked you about getting into heaven."

Sarah started to reply to her comment, but decided it should wait until another time. She thanked her and left the apartment, locking the door behind her.

Fred was not at the counter when she left. Even though it was after eight, it was almost as hot as earlier. At least - since it was late August, it would only be a few weeks until fall. Luckily her wait for the bus was short. Within twenty minutes, she was back at the home she shared with her mother. As she entered the house, she prayed that her mother would be asleep, or at least too engrossed in one of her romance novels, to hear her come in. That was not the case.

"Sarah, is that you?" she called from the living room as Sarah walked down the hallway.

"Yes, Mother," she answered. "Were you expecting someone else?" she asked, knowing her Mother had not had a visitor in months.

"Did you get my cigarettes?" her mother asked as she turned down the TV.

"I'm sorry, Mother," she answered as she stood in the doorway. "I haven't had a chance to stop anywhere. I'll get them tomorrow."

"You didn't have time to do anything for your mother, but you always have time to help complete strangers. Why don't you just say you don't want me to have cigarettes?"

"I have said it, Mother - at least a dozen times, for whatever good it's done. But I also told you I would buy them for you. I was just too tired to get them tonight. I'll go tomorrow."

"Fine," she responded nastily as she pointed the controller toward the T.V. and raised the volume. Sarah shook her head wearily and walked to her bedroom.

Sarah showered, brushed her teeth, and readied herself for bed. From her nightstand she took a novel she had been reading and climbed into bed. Although she tried to concentrate, her mind kept wandering to other matters. She thought about what Bertie had said. How did she know if she had been good enough to get to heaven? It was true that she had spent her entire life supporting her mother. And it was true that she always helped others in need. But, if the truth were known, her heart was not in it - at least not for the past few years. Her deeds were now done more out of ritual than out of compassion for others. That was a frightening thought. By her own words, God judged people by what was in their heart. What if all of her good works were in vain because they were not done for the right reasons?

Many thoughts floated through her head, but she was too tired to dwell on them. She soon placed the book on the nightstand, turned off the light, and tried to fall asleep. Tomorrow would be another long and trying day.

During the next two weeks, Sarah only visited Bertie Philpot on one occasion. This was because one of Bertie's sons, Jack, had taken a week off work to visit his mother. Even though Sarah enjoyed the rest - she was accustomed to volunteering at the home a couple of evenings a week - she did miss her conversations with her new friend. And although she had only known Bertie for a short time, it seemed as if they were old friends. She agreed with Fred Meade that Bertie was indeed a "character." She also soon discovered that, although she might be a little "peculiar," she certainly was in control of all her faculties. Sarah felt that, in time, she could learn much from her new friend.

In her last visit, Bertie had not mentioned their previous conversation about getting into heaven. Sarah never could find the proper time to bring it up and, before she realized it, the evening was over.

Sarah had hoped, since she was spending more time at home the last couple of weeks, that her mother would be less critical. That was not the case. Although her mother had always been a very trying and demanding person, it seemed, within the past few months, that she had become even more so. Although she had given it much thought, Sarah did not know the reason. Perhaps it was old age - she would be seventy in the fall. Perhaps, as she had claimed for many years, her health was failing. Although the doctors had confirmed that she had a mild case of arthritis, it was not as severe as experienced by many other people her age. And they could find no cause for the frequent headaches of which she complained. For whatever the reason for her increased complaints, it was very upsetting to Sarah to have spent her entire life supporting her mother and now to be shown such little appreciation.

It was Monday when Sarah received the call from the social worker asking if she could visit Mrs. Philpot the following evening. She eagerly accepted.

On the way to the home, Sarah wondered if this would be the evening Fred Meade would ask her for a date. He had seemed even more nervous than normal the last time she had spoke to him. He had begun to ask her more personal questions - like what she enjoyed doing in her spare time, or if she enjoyed traveling. Even so, he'd still not asked her for a date. Even if he did, she was still not certain what her answer would be. She'd thought much about what Bertie had said - that she should have a life of her own. But she could still not change her circumstances, and she knew that no man wanted a woman who was a nursemaid to an aging and spiteful mother. And, at her age, she wasn't sure she had the energy or desire to enter into a relationship. She decided it was probably her imagination anyway - he probably had no intention of asking her out.

As usual, Fred was behind the counter. He looked up and smiled as she entered the lobby. But it was a more thoughtful, if not serious, smile. She wondered if something was wrong.

"Hi, Fred," she said. "How are you this evening?"

"Oh, pretty good, Sarah. How was your day?" he asked.

"Tiring, as always. How's Bertie?"

"Oh, she's fine. Her son just left Saturday, so I guess she's not too happy about that, but she always bounces back."

"Yeah, she seems pretty resilient," she said as she set her bag on the counter. "Is something wrong?"

"Oh, no," he answered quickly. "Why?"

"Oh I don't mean to pry," she said. "You just seem, well, kind of serious."

He looked at her more thoughtfully as he walked closer.

"I've just got a lot on my mind," he stated. "My brother lives in Chattanooga. He's had a small supermarket down there for over twenty-five years. Well, he just turned sixty this year, so he plans to retire. He wants me to come down there and take over the business."

"That sounds like a good opportunity," said Sarah. "Do you want to do it?"

"I would make a lot more than I do here, and it wouldn't take too long to learn the business. My brother would still be around to help, but it would still be a big change and a lot of responsibility. Of course, I would also be closer to my daughter, and I have no other family here. But I like my job here, and I consider this my home. As you can see, I've been driving myself crazy for the past couple of days."

"It's a tough decision. So you don't know what you'll do?"

"Oh, I'll probably do it. I never could say no to him. And, as I said, it's a great opportunity."

"When does he want you to start?"

"As soon as possible. Unless I change my mind, I'll put in my notice tomorrow."

"Well, I'm happy for you Fred," said Sarah. She felt a touch of sadness at his announcement. She smiled, picked up her bag, and turned to walk away. "I think your brother's business will be in good hands."

As she started toward the elevator, Fred called to her. "Sarah," he said. "Can I ask you a question?"

"Sure," she answered as she turned toward him.

"You told me before that you like football, right?"

"Well, yeah. I'm not as big a fanatic as a lot of people around here but, yes, I enjoy football. Why?"

"Well," he began nervously, "I have two tickets to UT's opening game in a couple of weeks, and I thought you might like to go. What do you think?"

"That's on a Saturday afternoon, right?"

"Yes."

"Well, that's nice of you Fred," she answered, "but I'm afraid

I have to work until three on Saturdays. But thanks for asking though."

"Oh, well," he said as his eyes turned downward. "It was just a thought."

"Sorry," she replied as she turned away again. She almost reached the elevator before turning back to him again.

"Well, can I ask you a question now?" she asked.

"Sure."

"I'm just curious - why did you wait until you decided to move away before you asked me out?"

"Oh," he answered sheepishly. "Well, as you can probably tell, Sarah, I'm not exactly a ladies man. It's not easy for me to do this."

"Well, Fred," she returned with a slight laugh, "you're talking to a forty-two-year-old woman who has had only two somewhat serious relationships in her whole life. I'm not exactly a swinger either. But I still don't understand why you waited until you were moving until you asked me out."

"That's easy. It's now or never. Sort of like, 'put up or shut up,' you know."

"Oh," she replied with a laugh and a nod of her head. "I guess I can understand that. But what if I said yes? It wouldn't make much sense, would it?"

"I guess I don't always do things logically, Sarah. Besides, Chattanooga is only a two-hour drive."

"Well," she said, "I understand what you're saying. I don't always do the sensible thing either."

"Well, then, how about some other time?"

"Fred," she said seriously, "I just don't think it's a good idea. You know my situation with my mother. And now, with you moving away, I just don't see any future in it. But I do appreciate your asking."

"Okay," he said as he backed away from the counter, embarrassed and rejected.

"Thanks," she said as she turned and walked to the elevator.

As with her previous visits, the door to Bertie's apartment was unlocked. Sarah gently rapped on the door. She immediately heard Bertie's faint response.

"It's open." Bertie lay on the couch, her head resting on a pillow, with a magazine in her hand. She greeted her visitor warmly as she entered.

"Well, hi, Missy," she said. "It's so good to see you again."

"It's good to see you, Bertie," returned Sarah, as she bent down to give her a hug. "How's the foot?"

"Oh, it's getting better. I get to take this darn thing off in another couple of weeks. I'll sure be glad. I don't get any exercise with this thing on, you know. Even an old lady like myself needs some exercise. And I'm tired of having to count on other people to do everything for me. Not that I don't appreciate you, Missy. You can come any time. I just wish I could get around by myself."

"I understand," said Sarah.

"Enough about me," she continued. "How have you been? I've sure missed you."

"Thank you. I've been fine. I've been busy, as always, but I've been fine."

The two continued chatting for the next few minutes. Bertie told her about her visit from her son. Since it had been impossible for his wife to leave work, he'd come alone. He'd again tried to convince her to move in with them, but she again had declined. He had remained a few days - long enough to make certain she was in good health, and then returned to North Carolina.

"I'm kind of hungry this evening," stated Bertie. "Do you mind fixing us some supper?"

"Sure, what would you like?"

"I have some fried chicken that my neighbor brought earlier," she replied. "You can just warm that up. And I believe there is some potato salad left."

As she had done twice before, Sarah prepared the meal, helped seat her friend at the table, and then waited for her to say the blessing. When finished, they began to eat, chatting between bites.

"So, Sarah," Bertie soon asked, "how's your mother?"

"Well," answered Sarah, "that's a good question. She seems to be getting more difficult and unhappy as time goes by. It seems, lately, that no matter what I do I can't please her. If I work too much or come here to visit you she complains."

"I reckon she wants to keep you to herself."

"But if I'm home she complains that I'm just sitting around. I just don't understand her. I wish I had your outlook. What's your secret?"

"Well, as Will Rogers said, most people are just about as happy as they make up their minds to be. But I'm sorry about your mother. I know that makes it rough on you. I'd say just do the best you can and try to ignore her criticisms. You've never said anything about your father. Is he alive?"

"No," she answered, "he died when I was only nine."

"Oh, I'm sorry, Missy. Do you remember much about him?"

"Oh, yes."

"You sure answered that in a hurry. Why do you say it like that?"

"Well, my father was a very - shall we say - self-righteous man."

"I see. So he wasn't the most pleasant person to live with?"

"Hardly. The thing I remember most about him was how he always found something wrong with anything my mother or I did. We could never seem to please him."

"That's sad. Maybe that's where your mother got it."

"Yes, I've thought about that, but more than likely, that's why they got married. They were well-suited to each other. And he loved to use his knowledge of the Bible to keep me in line."

"What type of things did he say?"

"Oh, you know - children should always honor their father and mother; spare the rod and spoil the child; the husband is the head of the family. Different things like that."

"That's sad," said Bertie. "It sounds like your father may have been familiar with the Bible but never really understood it."

"Why do you say that?"

"Well, for example, dear," answered Bertie, "even though the Bible does say 'spare the rod and spoil the child,' it doesn't mean you're supposed to use a rod to beat children. In Biblical times, the rod was used by shepherds to guide and direct the flock, not beat them. The Bible also says that we are also supposed to discern the word. That means it's our duty to study the word to understand what God meant."

"That's really interesting," replied Sarah. "I never heard any of that before. I knew I could learn a lot from you."

"Well," she replied with a laugh, "I reckon I've been around long enough. It'd be a shame if I hadn't a learned something by now."

The two continued their conversation as they ate. Soon, they finished their meal and Sarah helped her friend back to the couch. She cleaned the table and placed the dishes in the dishwasher. She then asked Bertie what other chores needed to be done.

"Oh, don't you fret about that," she replied, "you're here to keep an old woman company. Come and sit down by me. I like talking to you."

Sarah joined her on the couch. Bertie immediately asked her if she had thought about her advice of living her own life. She told her of her conversation with Fred Meade.

"Well, if you don't mind an old lady giving you her opinion," stated Bertie, "I think you should go out with him. He's a real nice man and I think he really likes you."

"But, Bertie," she objected, "it just doesn't make sense. Even if we found out we liked each other, it wouldn't work out. He's moving away and - even though he may not admit it - my relationship with my mother would eventually be a big problem. I just don't think it would work."

Bertie studied her a moment before speaking.

"Well do you know what I think, Missy?" she asked. "I don't

think that's what's bothering you. I think you just don't believe you deserve any happiness in life. I'm sorry for being so blunt, but I'm an old woman and I don't have a lot of time to be tactful. Your father was wrong. He used God's word to frighten and punish you. And even though we are supposed to be obedient to God, it's more important to know that He loves us and wants us to be joyful in Him. I think you're still trying to live up to your father's idea of how you should be living your life."

Sarah stared blankly at the floor, contemplating what her friend had said. She soon looked back at Bertie and spoke.

"Bertie, although I appreciate your concern, I have to tell you that I don't agree with you."

"Well, Missy," she answered, "I reckon it won't be the first time I've been wrong, and hopefully not the last. But that's what I think."

"I only told you about my father - I didn't tell you about me. I know this will be a surprise to you, but I was not always the type of person you see today. You see, I was a very difficult and stubborn child - at least that's what my father used to say. Although it's true the things I told you about him, I never agreed with the things he said. I was a very headstrong and rebellious little girl. Because of that I really don't think my problems are because of him."

"If that's the case then, Missy" returned Bertie, "what made you change? It doesn't take a genius to see that you're not like that today."

Sarah looked at her friend for a moment, pondering her question. She then turned away, took a deep breath, and began to speak softly.

"Bertie, what I am about to say I've never told another person. And I don't know why, but I've been thinking a lot about it lately. I want you to know I'm only telling you this because I trust you and respect your opinion."

Bertie reached forward and patted her hand.

"Go ahead, dear."

"When I was very young - about three or four I think - a young

THE GREATEST GIFT   151

couple moved in next door to us. They had a little girl the same age
as me. Actually I was almost a year older but we started school at
the same time and were in the same class. Elizabeth and I became
best friends. Unlike me, she was a very sweet and obedient little
girl. I guess the only time she ever got into trouble was when I was
around. I think that's why I liked her so much - I could always talk
her into doing whatever I wanted. Now I don't want you to think
that I was ever mean to her because I wasn't - I guess I just liked
the idea of her thinking of me as being her leader. My father was
always punishing me for getting her in trouble. He kept telling me
what a bad influence I was."

Bertie saw the sadness in her friend's face as she told the story.
She waited patiently for her to continue.

"It was the winter before my father died that it happened. I was
eight and Lizzy - that's what I called her - was seven. It was a cold,
snowy day in January. School had closed because of the storm, but
both my mother and father had to go to work. Since Lizzy's mother
didn't work, my mother said I could spend the day with them. We
spent the morning playing in her room and watching TV. I guess it
was about eleven that her Mother came in and said she needed to
run down to the store to pick up a few things for lunch. We asked
if we could stay home alone. She didn't like the idea of leaving us,
but, since it was so cold, and since she would only be gone less than
an hour, she finally gave in. She instructed us to not leave the house
or open the door for anybody."

Bertie could see that it was getting more difficult for Sarah to
continue. However, she decided to say nothing, giving her the time
she needed to tell her story.

"Well, of course," she continued, "as soon as her mother had
left, I convinced Lizzy to go into the woods behind her house to
make a snowman. I was pretty smart. I knew that if we made one
in her yard they would obviously know we had been out of the
house. But, since the woods were only a couple hundred feet away,
we would have time to make a snowman and return and no one

would be the wiser. She was against it but, as always, it didn't take much convincing.

"We bundled up and ran to the woods, and forgot about the little stream that ran along the edge of her property. We couldn't see it because of the snow, and Lizzy tripped and fell in the water up to her knees. She started crying, so I helped her up and we went back into the house. I was pretty clever. We took her clothes off - even her boots - and put them in the dryer. Her mother was gone longer than expected so by the time she returned, everything was back to normal. As far as I know, she never knew what happened."

"That's an interesting story, sweetie," said Bertie, "but I don't see how such an event could have any impact on someone's life."

"That's not the end of the story," said Sarah as she removed a tissue from her purse and blew her nose. "The next day, Lizzy was not at school. I went by her house later and was told by her mother that she had a very bad cold. Well, to make the story short, within a few days it turned into pneumonia and she died."

Bertie placed her hand on her friend's shoulder as she bent her head forward and sobbed.

"I didn't find out until later that she had had previous problems with her lungs. I never told anyone what happened. I was afraid of what my father would do."

Bertie said nothing, but leaned forward and placed her arm around Sarah. She let her continue to cry for a while longer before speaking.

"That's a terrible thing to have kept to yourself all these years."

"Yes," she cried.

"And to blame yourself for your friend's death. That is a terrible burden to bear - especially since you were not responsible."

"How can you say that?" she answered angrily. "I know that Lizzy would be alive today if I hadn't convinced her to go outside."

"You were a little child," returned Bertie, "a little child who wanted to play in the snow. And you knew nothing about your friend's illness. I'm glad you are finally able to talk about it, but you can't hold yourself responsible."

"I appreciate your kindness," said Sarah, "but no matter what you say, my friend would be alive today if not for me."

The two sat without speaking. Soon, Sarah was able to control her sobbing and turned to look at her friend. Bertie smiled wearily. For the first time since she had known her, Bertie looked her age.

"Are you okay?" asked Sarah. "You look awful tired."

"I am a little weary," she answered. "It's because of this darn cast. I can't move around so I don't get much circulation. I'll be fine though."

Bertie thought for a minute before continuing. "Okay, dear," she continued. "Let's look at it your way. Even if your actions did cause your friend's death, we both know it wasn't intentional."

"I know that. But it still doesn't remove the pain."

"Have you asked God to forgive you?"

"Well, I'm obviously not as religious as you, Bertie, but, yes, I've prayed about it."

"But you need to actually ask Him to forgive you. And then, just as important, you have to forgive yourself."

"Unfortunately, that's easier said than done."

"I know," returned her friend as she patted her hand once more.

Sarah again looked at her friend who now had her eyes closed. She became concerned for her.

"Are you sure you are all right, Bertie?"

"Oh, of course I am," she returned as she opened her eyes. "It's just as I said - I get tired real easy lately. I'm really sorry, Missy. You've just opened your heart to me and I know how you're hurting, but I'm afraid I will have to wait until our next visit to continue. Is that okay?"

"Of course it is. I just appreciate your listening. It feels good to finally talk to someone about this."

She helped her friend up and walked with her to her bed.

"I just want to say one more thing," said Bertie as she helped her into bed. "When we talk next time I'll have some good news for you."

"How's that?" she asked.

"That's all I will say for now," she returned. "But you just try to quit worrying for awhile and I'll explain next time. Can you come by tomorrow?"

"I have to work tomorrow evening. How about Thursday?"

"That will be great, my dear. And we'll have a good talk then."

She helped her friend get ready for bed, then closed and locked the door behind her, and caught the bus for home.

During the next two days, Sarah spent much of her time thinking of her conversation with Bertie. Telling her of the incident with Lizzy brought back feelings and memories she had tried to forget. And now she wondered if the incident had impacted her even more than she'd realized. To show remorse over her friend's death, had she dedicated her life to helping others? Was she filled with such guilt that she subconsciously felt she didn't deserve any happiness? Was that the real reason she had refused to go out with Fred? And, more curiously, how could she not even know the answer to these questions - how could she not know her own self, her own motivations? She decided that she was probably being overly dramatic. She was probably only a victim of life's circumstances. It was true that she had spent most of her life taking care of her mother, but then wasn't that what a daughter was supposed to do? And, so what if she had never married - she had had relationships with men. They had just never worked out.

But one thing was certain - her actions had led to her little friend's death. It was just as her father had always said - her stubbornness would cause a real problem some day. Only the "problem" had not been hers - and it had been much worse than anyone could ever realize.

She wondered what the "good news" was which Bertie spoke of? She couldn't imagine what her friend could tell her that could change anything. But, she had to admit, she was very eager - perhaps even desperate, to hear what her friend had to say.

———————

The weather had cooled considerably in the past couple of weeks. There were only a few days remaining in August, and the temperature had only climbed into the mid-eighties today. Sarah felt that the weather was perhaps responsible for her increased energy this evening. She did not even mind standing at the bus stop as she began her trip to the senior citizens center.

As usual, the bus arrived in front of the apartment building just before six o'clock. Sarah walked briskly toward the lobby, apprehensive about talking to Fred Meade. She had been thining about asking him if he still wanted to go out, but still had not decided if it was the right thing to do. Perhaps when she saw him the answer would come to her.

Fred was not behind the counter when she arrived. Instead, there was a woman unfamiliar to her. She was a heavy set, Black woman who appeared to be in her mid-fifties. Sarah walked to the counter and introduced herself.

"Hi," she began, "I'm Sarah Horton. I'm a volunteer."

"Oh, hi, Sarah," she responded, "I'm Lucy Honeycutt. I'm usually on the day shift around here. I guess you're used to dealing with Fred."

"Yes. Did he leave already?"

"No. He just took the day off to go to Chattanooga. He's moving there, you know."

"Yes. He told me," she said as she set her bag on the floor. "I guess he and his brother have a lot of things to work out."

"I'm sure they do. Now what can I do for you this evening? You've come to spend some time with one of our tenants, right?"

"Yes, Bertie Philpot. You know her?"

The look in the woman's eyes immediately told her that something was wrong.

"What's wrong?" asked Sarah.

"I'm sorry, dear," Mrs. Honeycutt answered slowly, "Bertie passed away last night. Someone should have called you, but I guess it was just overlooked. I'm terribly sorry."

Sarah was overcome with shock and sorrow. In a trance, she picked up her bag and walked to a nearby chair. Mrs. Honeycutt left the counter and came to her.

"I'm terribly sorry. Were you and her very close?"

"Yes," Sarah answered as she slowly nodded her head. "Oh, we had only known each other a short time, but - well, yes, we were very close."

"I wish there was something I could do. Let me go get you some water."

Mrs. Honneycutt returned soon with a glass of water. Sarah took a sip and turned back to her.

"What happened?" she asked.

"I hope this doesn't sound insensitive," she answered, "but I don't really know. We deal with death here almost every week, you know. When somebody gets to that age things just wear out. If it makes any difference, though, I know it happened quickly so she didn't suffer."

"Okay," said Sarah, staring blankly into the cup.

"You just sit there and rest," said Mrs. Honeycutt. "If I can get you anything else, please let me know."

The woman patted her on her shoulder, then turned and walked away. Sarah sat quietly, thinking of her friend. She knew how much she would miss her. She was amazed that, even though they had only known each other for such a short time, they had grown so close. And now she would never know what "good news" Bertie had for her. She sat silently for a few minutes, then, realizing she could do nothing there, arose to leave. As she did so she noticed a well-dressed man speaking to Mrs. Honeycutt. He appeared to be in his mid-fifties. Leaving the counter, he walked towards her. As he neared Sarah he held out his hand.

"You're Ms. Horton, right?" he asked.

"Yes," she responded as she took his hand.

"I'm Jack Philpot, Bertie's son."

"Oh," she said as she grasped his hand. "It's so nice to meet you."

"No, it's nice to meet you," he said." In fact, it's a real honor to meet you. My mother talked an awful lot about you. I can't thank you enough for everything you've done."

"It was my pleasure. Your mother is - uh, was - a wonderful woman. I've learned a lot from her. I should be thanking you for the time I've spent with her. I can't tell you how much I'm going to miss her."

The two talked for a couple more minutes. Jack explained that he had just learned of his mother's death earlier that morning, and had immediately flown into town to take care of her affairs. He had just left her apartment when they met. He told her that the rest of the family would be arriving the next day, then he invited Sarah to the services which were to be held on Saturday. Sarah explained that she would attempt to get off work and attend. He again thanked her for her kindness and turned to leave. He then quickly turned back to her, removing an envelope from his pocket and handing it to Sarah.

"I'm terribly sorry," he said. "I'm not thinking too clearly and almost forgot this. Evidently my mother left it for you."

It was a plain white envelope with the words, "My Good Friend Sarah" written on it.

"Thanks," she said as she stared at the envelope and sat down. Jack smiled and walked away.

She sat holding the envelope for a moment. She had many questions as she studied the envelope. Why would Bertie have written her a letter unless she knew she would not see her again?

And how could she have been that ill and Sarah never know? And, obviously, what was so important that a dying woman would spend her last day writing to a new friend. The answers to the questions could only be found in the envelope. She briefly thought of waiting for the privacy of her room to read the letter, but quickly realized she could not do so. She gently opened the letter and began to read.

My dear Sarah,

If you're reading this letter it means I have gone to be with my husband. Now don't start feeling sorry for me - I've had a good and long life and have no fear of death. I'm kind of looking forward to what heaven will be like. If you're curious about why I'm writing this letter now - well, I didn't want to worry you, but my heart has been acting up a bit lately so I never know if I'll be around from one day till the next. Anyway, this letter isn't about me, it's about you.

I'm sorry I couldn't finish our conversation yesterday. There were many things I wanted to say to you. That's why I'm writing this letter.

The first thing I want to tell you is this. I told you to ask God to forgive you for what happened to your friend Lizzy. Well, I can assure you that if you asked for forgiveness then you were forgiven. Jesus told us that we are to forgive others just as God forgives us. The problem is that when people are overcome with guilt they won't forgive themselves. Well, that's wrong Missy. If God forgives you not only should you forgive yourself, but God COMMANDS us to forgive ourselves. Or else, we're putting ourselves above Him. So the first thing you have to do is get rid of this guilt. And that's not from me but a direct order from God.

But I think there's something more important that you need to know. I think because of everything that's happened to you - the situation with Lizzy, as well as your problems with your mother and father - you have a bad misunderstanding about something.

To be blunt, Missy, you can't work your way into heaven. In God's eyes we're all sinners and none of our good deeds will get us into heaven. As the Bible says, "For by grace are ye saved through faith; and that not of yourselves; it is the gift of God: not of works, least any man should boast."

So to pay for our sins, God took on human flesh in the form of Jesus, died in man's place, and rose to demonstrate victory over death. The Bible says, "For He hath made Christ to be sin for us, who knew no sin, that we might be made the righteousness of God in Him."

It's as simple as that Missy. All you have to do is to trust in Jesus to receive eternal life. If we could get into heaven by doing good works then Jesus would have died in vain. Now that doesn't mean that you shouldn't be doing all your good deeds - it's just that you've got the cart a little before the horse. Once you put your faith in Jesus, you then try and live the life He wants. But then you don't have to worry about being "good enough" to get into heaven.

Well, that's about all I have to say Missy. I can't tell you what decisions to make in your life, but I know you'll do what's right. I hope I'll get to tell you these things in person, but if I don't, I just want you to know what a joy and comfort you've been to me in the short time we've know each other. I hope my words - or should I say "God's Words" - will provide comfort to you as they have to me.

Thank you and God bless you.
Your friend, Bertie

Tears filled Sarah's eyes as she finished the letter. What a remarkable woman she had been. She thought about what she had told her. It truly was, as Bertie had said, "good news." Even though her father had claimed to know the Bible - and even though she had attended church many times in her life, she was still not aware of what Bertie had just said. She lowered her head and asked Jesus to come into her life.

She soon raised her head, wiped the tears from her face, arose and walked toward the door. She eagerly waited for the bus to take her home. There were many things she had to do. She would first have to have a long talk with her mother. She would then have to find a good church. And tomorrow, if it were not too late, she had to call a friend about going out to dinner.

BEFORE THE FALL

The center held up his hand signaling the other players to gather around. Once the chatter had died down, the quarterback for the Denver Highlanders, Vick Carpenter, looked around at his teammates. "Okay, guys, we've got to have this third down. It may be our last chance. Let's go with spot 17, outside in."

"I can beat my guy to the post," said wide receiver Terry Tibbetts.

"That's too risky. We just need seven yards," said Carpenter.

"And that's what they're expecting. I'm telling you, I can beat him. Just get me the ball."

"Just listen to your quarterback," snapped Craig Lovett, center and team captain.

Tibbetts stared at Lovett but said nothing. "Okay," said Carpenter, "Here's what we're going to do. Everybody run spot 17, but Terry, you hit the post. I'll pump once across the middle, and then hit you if you got your man beat."

"That ain't gonna be a problem."

The team came up to the line. Carpenter looked at the clock. There were less than two minutes remaining in the game, and they were on their own forty-seven yard line. Trailing by only two points, they needed to get inside Detroit's thirty yard line for a reasonable shot at a field goal. With two seconds on the play clock, Lovett snapped the ball. Carpenter took the snap and dropped back. Detroit's all-pro linebacker, Lionel Williams, shot across the line and took aim on Carpenter, but was cut down at the last second by the running back. The tight end, who had lined up on the left side, ran full speed for ten yards, faked an outside move and cut to the center of the field. Carpenter faked a pass to him. As they had hoped, the safety took the fake and moved toward the line. Tibbetts, at full speed, turned to the inside and headed towards the goal post. Carpenter let the ball go, just before being leveled by a 300-pound defensive lineman.

Tibbetts had his man beat by five yards and knew he had a touchdown - until he realized the ball was underthrown. Slowing down for the ball, he leapt for it at the same time as the defender. Tibbetts caught the ball in one hand and pulled it to his chest. As he came down, he twisted and tried to pull away from the defender, who was falling to the ground. Just when he thought he was free, his opponent grasped his shoulder pad and pulled him to the ground. He landed with a thud on his shoulder and head. As he jumped to his feet, he felt a sharp pain in his shoulder. The defender sneered at him as if to say, "Got you, didn't I?" Tibbetts threw the ball and hit the opponent's helmet. When he moved toward Tibbetts he raised his foot and kicked him in the leg. Immediately the referee was between the two men. He pulled his flag and threw it on the ground, then turned to Tibbetts and yelled, "Fifteen yards, personal foul."

"What are you talking about?" yelled Tibbetts.

"Fifteen yards," repeated the referee.

The referee turned to walk away, but Tibbetts put his hand on his shoulder and said, "Ump, why are you calling it on me? He's the one…"

The referee turned immediately and yelled, "You're out of the game! And don't ever put your hand on an official again!"

"I was just trying to get your attention," said Tibbetts as the referee turned his back.

The crowd hissed and booed as Tibbetts stood watching the referee walk away. Soon the offensive coordinator came and led him off the field. Once at the sideline, a security guard came and escorted him toward the dressing room. The head coach, Roy Dillon, only stared as he walked by.

Tibbetts reached the deserted locker room, threw his helmet against the lockers, and sat on the bench. He sat nursing his anger for a while, then slowly got undressed and took a shower. From the sounds of the crowd above, it appeared that the Highlanders had scored. He had just finishing dressing when he again heard the roar of the crowd, which he knew meant a victory for his team. Soon, the players stormed into the room yelling and shouting, "We're in the playoffs!" A few players stopped to greet Tibbetts and offer their sympathy for being thrown out of the game, but most passed him by. Soon the coaches entered the room to congratulate the players. Coach Dillon's speech was short and to the point.

"Good game today, men. That's the best you've played all year. We're in the playoffs, but let's win these last two games for home field advantage. Go home and spend time with your families and we'll see you Tuesday."

After talking to a few players, Tibbetts picked up his gym bag and left the locker room. The press would be allowed in the locker room after the players had showered, but he had nothing to say to them. He was tired of their personal attacks. As he was leaving through a side door, he ran into one of the assistant coaches.

"Coach Dillon wants to see you in his office," he said as he walked by.

Tibbetts turned to ask why, but he had already passed him by, headed down the stairs. Tibbetts went to his car and threw his gym bag in the trunk, then walked to coach Dillon's office. The coach looked up from his desk and saw Tibbetts standing at his doorway.

"You wanted to see me?" asked Tibbetts.

"Have a seat," said the coach as he waved his hand to a chair in front of his desk.

Tibbetts walked slowly to the chair and threw himself in it.

"What did you want to talk about?"

"That was some performance you put on out there this afternoon."

"Yeah?"

"Kicking a player, then putting your hands on the umpire."

"I was just trying to get his attention. No big deal."

"I guess he didn't agree. And that's what - the third game you've been kicked out of this year?"

"I play hard, coach. You know that."

"That's no excuse, Terry, and I'm tired of having these conversations with you. Every game it's something. You're either fighting with another player - sometimes even one of your own teammates - or your alienating the referees."

"Like I said, I'm an intense player. That's what makes me the best receiver in the league. You got to take the bad with good."

"Yeah, well I think the bad has about outweighed the good. I'll make it simple. I'm not waiting to see what the league might do. You're suspended for the final two games."

"What? Are you crazy? If we don't win the last two games then we don't have home field advantage for the playoffs. And you know you can't do that without me."

"I'll take that chance. Talk to you in two weeks."

With his last statement Coach Dillon lowered his head and started reading a letter on his desk. Tibbetts sat silently for a moment, then arose and pushed the chair away and walked out the door.

———

Terry Tibbetts walked hurriedly to his car, a new Corvette, and within minutes was on Interstate 70, headed to his home in the

Rocky Mountains. His mind was on the game and his conversation with coach Dillon. How could he be so narrow-minded and critical? If not for his play the Highlanders wouldn't have even made the playoffs. There was a reason why his license plate read TNT-10. But now, because of one little incident, he was suspended for the last two games. It would serve them right if they lost both games.

He was deep in thought when he looked up to see a Colorado State Trooper behind him, red lights flashing. He waited for it to go around, but instead it pulled closer to his car. He pulled his Corvette to the side of the road and waited. Tapping his fingers on the steering wheel, he watched as a black State Trooper exited the car, put on his hat, and walked to his window. Tibbetts rolled down the window. "What's the problem, Officer?"

"Your license and registration, please."

Tibbetts removed his license from his wallet and took the registration from the glove compartment and handed it to the trooper. He continued to tap his fingers on the steering wheel as he waited for the trooper to comment. Finally the officer asked, "You in a big hurry today, Mr. Tibbetts?"

"No, not really, why? Was I speeding?"

"Eighty-five in a sixty-five."

"I didn't really notice. I just got the car and it's a lot smoother than my SUV."

"Guess you should have taken that into account, sir," he said as he took out his book and began to write a ticket.

"You're not really going to give me a ticket are you, Brother?"

The Trooper looked at him over the top of his sunglasses. "Yes, Sir, and, far as I know, we're not related."

"Come on now," answered Tibbetts. "Do you know who I am?"

"Sure do. You're the man who I just clocked doing eighty-five in a sixty-five."

Tibbetts started to respond but, seeing the look in the trooper's eyes, decided against it.

"Have a nice day," said the officer as he handed him the ticket and walked away.

"Probably a Detroit fan," thought Tibbetts to himself as he threw the ticket in the seat and pulled back onto the interstate.

Twenty minutes later he pulled into the long, winding driveway of his Rocky Mountain home. He parked his Corvette in the three-car garage, and walked through the laundry room into the kitchen. Standing over the stove, stirring a pot, was his mother.

"Hi, Mom," he said.

"Hi, Terry."

"Whatcha cooking?"

"Spaghetti sauce. I thought you and Jacob might enjoy some for dinner."

"Sounds good. Has Sophia called?"

"No, but I'm sure they will be back by six o'clock, just like she said."

"Oh, okay," he said as he took a spoon from the drawer and sampled the spaghetti.

"It's not ready for another ten minutes," said his mother.

"Still tastes good."

He put the spoon in the sink and turned and walked away. He went a few feet then turned back to his mother.

"So, did you see the game?"

"I saw it."

"And?"

After staring at him for a second, she answered. "You played a great game as always, Terry."

"It sounds like there's something else you want to say."

"No need to go into it again."

"If there's something you want to say then you should say it, Mom."

"Okay. Then I wish you would learn to control your temper, then maybe you wouldn't get thrown out of so many games."

"It's a tough game, Mom, and you know how much I like to

win. Besides, you saw how the safety threw me to the ground. He was trying to bust my shoulder so I couldn't play."

"And what about the referee? Was there a need to attack him?"

"I didn't attack him. I was just trying to get him to listen to me," he answered as he shook his head. "You're right - I guess we shouldn't have this conversation."

Terry started toward his bedroom, then again stopped and turned back toward his mother.

"You know what I don't understand, Mom?"

"What?"

"When I was growing up, you and dad both told me that I should be proud. You said that no other person, black or white, was better than me. Now, that I live like you taught me, I find out you really don't believe that. I guess it was just words."

"No, it's not just words, Terry, but you took it one step further. We never told you that you were better than everybody else. God made all people equal. There's not one race or color better than another. That's what your father and I were saying to you. How do you think he would feel about the way you're acting if he were alive today?"

She waited for an answer but, receiving none, continued. "The Bible says that pride goes before a fall."

He looked at her for a second, opened his mouth to speak, then shook his head and left for his bedroom.

It was half past five when the doorbell rang. From his bedroom Terry heard his mother open the door, then heard the voices of his son and ex-wife. Terry walked from his bedroom into the foyer. His seven-year-old son, Jacob, ran and hugged his father.

"Hi, Dad," he greeted him.

"Glad you're back home, Son," said Terry. "Did you have a nice time at Latisha's party?"

"Oh, yeah, it was great."

"Did you get to watch my game?"

"Only for a minute, Dad. Aunt Danielle doesn't have a TV in the play room."

Terry shot his ex-wife a quick look of dissatisfaction. She quickly turned to his mother and began talking.

"Well," continued Terry, "I recorded the game and was just going over it. You want to go watch it with me while Grandma gets dinner ready?"

"That sounds great, Dad." Jacob ran and gave his mother a hug and thanked her for taking him to the party, then ran down the hall toward the den.

Terry turned to follow his son when Sophia called to him.

"Terry, can we talk about something?"

"What's that?"

His mother turned and went back toward the kitchen as Sophia walked closer to him.

"Terry, I wish you would reconsider letting Jacob live with me. It would be a lot better for him."

"It's not going to happen."

"It's a lot better for a boy to be with his mother. And besides, you travel half the time."

"I have eight away games a year."

"Plus four weeks of spring training, and usually two or three weeks of playoffs. He would really be better off with me."

"Guess you should have thought of that before you left, huh?"

"Before I left I wasn't allowed any thoughts of my own."

The anger in his eyes told her that maybe she had gone to far. He turned to walk away. She put her hand on his arm.

"I'm sorry, that was nasty. I wish you would at least consider it."

"If the judge had thought it was in Jacob's best interest, he would have had him live with you."

"And the fact that you had the best lawyers money could buy had nothing to do with it? All I'm asking is that you think about it."

"Fine, I'll think about it. Anything else?"

"I guess not," she answered as she turned and walked out the door.

———————————

Terry joined his son in the den. They watched the game together, Jacob cheering at every catch his father made. Soon the play that got him ejected came up. Terry said nothing but observed his son as he watched the game.

"Oh, wow, Dad," he shouted, "I can't believe he threw you out of the game. That really stinks."

"I think so too, Son. Nothing I can do now though."

"I bet it wouldn't have happened if the referee had been black."

His son's comments surprised him. "I don't know, Son. There are idiots of all colors. He just made a bad call."

"Oh, okay, Dad. You'll show 'em next time."

———————————

Early the next morning Terry's mother arose and left for her job at a nursing home in Denver. It was a little after nine when Terry returned home from dropping his son off at school. He changed into his sweatsuit, went into his exercise room, and began his routine. That was one of the things that made him the best receiver in the NFL - his dedication and work ethic. Most players would wait two, even three days after a game before exercising, but he began the day after. Of course, today would be a light workout - just enough to stretch his muscles and keep himself limber. At age twenty-seven he was still young, and it was his attitude that would keep him the best receiver in the game for years to come. And if Coach Dillon didn't appreciate him, there were plenty of other teams that wanted him, probably for more money.

He was deep in thought when his doorbell rang. He put a towel around his neck and walked to the front door. Peering out the peephole he saw an unfamiliar middle-aged white man dressed in a suit. Terry opened the door.

"Can I help you?"

"Yes, Mr. Tibbetts," said the visitor. "My name is Samuel Powell, and I just put a contract on the house next door to you. It looks like we'll be neighbors."

"Oh, you're buying the Jacksons' house?"

"Yes, sir. They just accepted the contract, so hopefully we will be moving in in a few weeks."

"Well, congratulations and welcome to the neighborhood."

"Thank you. However, there is one little problem I need to talk to you about."

"What's that?"

The man rubbed his hands together as he looked around before turning back to Terry.

"Well, the survey just came back and, well, it seems that part of your fence is on the Jackson's property."

"On their property?" he repeated. "I had it surveyed just before I bought the place three years ago, and the fence company used the survey to put up the fence."

"I'm sure, but the realtor and I had them do it twice to make sure, and there's no mistake. But it's not a really big problem. The fence is only over a couple of feet on one end. And it's at an angle so it's only a total of about twenty to thirty square feet - not a big difference for lots as big as these."

"And just exactly what do you want me to do about this?"

"Well, sir...uh, Mr. Tibbetts, the realtor said there are two possibilities. We can have the deed corrected to show the extra few feet belong to you..."

"That sounds good."

"Well, the only problem with that is that it'll take time and our settlement date will be moved back."

"Then I guess that is what you will have to do."

"But, Mr. Tibbetts, there is another simple solution."

"What's that?"

"Well, you could just move the fence a couple of feet."

"That's not going to happen."

"Sir, if it's a question of money, I'm sure we could work something out."

"Money is not the issue. It's my property and I already have a survey that says so. You just get the deed corrected."

"But sir, like I told you, that will take a lot of time, and my wife and I have to move in as soon as possible. Won't you please be reasonable?"

"I am being reasonable. Now that's all I have to say about it. Understand?"

Mr. Powell moved closer to Terry and put his hand on his arm.

"Please, Mr. Tibbetts, you don't know how important this is to my wife and me. Won't you please re-consider?"

"Don't put your hands on me!" said Terry as he turned to go.

Powell followed behind, pleading for him to change his mind. As Terry grabbed the screen door to pull it closed, Powell put his foot in the door. Terry looked down at his foot, then pushed the door open. He grabbed Powell by his shoulder and threw him to the ground. The man lay for a second, then got up slowly holding his shoulder. He stared at Terry, but said nothing, then turned and walked hurriedly toward his car. Terry watched from the door as the man placed his cell phone to his ear and began talking. He then backed out of his driveway and drove away.

"Fool!" said Terry aloud as he closed the door. "The man has to be crazy. Trying to force himself into my house."

He paced up and down the hallway, thinking of what had just happened. Why was the man so insistent that he move the fence? It wasn't his problem that the surveyor screwed up. Maybe it was his surveyor who made the mistake. And why should he pay for it anyway? It wasn't about the extra few feet of land, it was the principle of the thing.

He went into the kitchen and poured himself another cup of

coffee. He sipped the coffee for a minute, then went into the bedroom and undressed and took a shower. He couldn't spend any more time worrying about it. He had to get on with his life.

He was watching films of his old games when the doorbell rang.

"It can't be the same idiot," he said as he walked to the door. He stopped and again looked at the peephole. There stood a large Hawaiian-looking deputy sheriff. Terry shook his head and opened the door.

"Mr. Tibbetts?" asked the deputy.

"Yes, Sir."

"I'm Deputy Waihee. Can I come in to talk to you?"

"I guess this is about my crazy new neighbor?"

"Yes - Mr. Powell. Can I come inside please?"

Terry moved aside and let the deputy enter. He led him into the living room where they sat.

"So, what did that crazy man say about me?"

"Actually, he filed a complaint against you. He said you broke his collarbone."

"You're kidding! And did he tell you that he tried to force his way into my house?"

"His version was a little different. That's why I'm here - to get at the truth."

Terry told him his version of what happened as the deputy listened patiently.

"The bottom line is, Deputy, that he tried to force his way into my house, and all I did was push him backwards and he fell. I don't think a man can be arrested for defending his house."

"Like I said, Mr. Tibbetts, his version is a little different. He said he only stepped onto your landing to plead with you, and you grabbed him and threw him to the ground."

"And you believe him? He put his foot in the door and tried to force his way inside."

"It's kind of hard to believe a little man like that would

try to push his way inside against someone as big and imposing as you."

"Well, that's what happened. What did you come here for? To arrest me?"

"Mr. Tibbetts, one thing I've learned on this job, is that the truth is probably somewhere between two peoples' versions of what happened. What I'm here for is to try and work this out so no one gets hurt."

"Again, that's what happened. So what's next?"

"I'll go back and talk to Mr. Powell again. He seems like a nice man. Maybe by then he'll have calmed down. And I guess we'll take it from there."

The deputy arose and walked toward the door, Terry accompanying him. Before leaving, however, he turned back to Terry with a slight smile.

"You don't remember me, do you?"

"Remember you? What do you mean?"

Terry studied the man's face for a second.

"You do look a little familiar, though. Where have I met you before?"

"We never formally met, however, we came in contact a few years ago when our two teams played."

"Oh, yes, now I remember. You played for the Trojans - linebacker."

"Yes, and you were an All-American receiver for the Bruins."

"Well, you should have been All-American. I can honestly say that you gave me some of the hardest tackles I ever had. How come you didn't go pro?"

"I busted my knee later that year. I thought I was fine after it healed, but I guess the NFL didn't agree."

"How did you end up here?"

"My wife is from Denver."

"And how did you end up being a cop....sorry, police officer?"

"My father was a cop in Honolulu, so I guess, when I couldn't play pro ball, I just followed in his footsteps."

"Well, good, I hope it turns out okay for you."

Terry held out his hand toward the deputy who shook it before turning again toward the door. Just before leaving, he again turned back to him.

"Mr. Tibbetts, I hope I'm not out of line here, but..."

"What?"

"This has nothing to do with why I'm here...well, maybe it does. Your father would not be happy with they way you have been acting the past few years."

"And you knew my father, too?"

"No, I didn't, but I read and heard a lot about him - how he was always giving of his time and money to help others."

"Oh, yes. There was more than one newspaper article about the Post Office employee who gave away half of his salary to others more in need."

"Yes, he was quite a man."

Terry looked around for a second, before turning back to the deputy.

"There's more than one side to every story, deputy."

"Meaning?"

"Meaning how do you think my mother and I were doing while he was giving away all his money and spending his time helping others?"

"I never really thought of that."

"Yeah, neither did anybody else. If I had't gotten a scholarship, I never would have gone to college and played pro ball. And when my father died, he left us penniless. If I hadn't gotten that big signing bonus, my mother would still be living in some little apartment in the ghetto in L.A."

"I see. No. I didn't know that. But, let me ask you one question. Who do you think has done more good in their life?"

"You sound like my mother. Always telling me I have too much pride. Always quoting the Bible to me about pride going before the fall. Well, my father didn't have any pride, so I guess I got his, too."

"Actually I think the verse goes, 'Pride goes before destruction, and a haughty spirit before a fall.'"

The deputy waited for a response, but received none. Before leaving, he had one other comment.

"Mr. Tibbetts, I'm sorry if I was out of line, but I thought I should give my opinion. And there's one other thing I think you should know. Mr. Powell didn't want me to tell you this, probably out of his own pride - or maybe embarrassment - but there's a reason why he didn't want to wait to have the deed changed. You see, his wife is dying of cancer. She only has a few weeks left, and her dream, since she was a little girl, was to have a house on a mountain where she could look down on the valley below. Anyway, just something I thought you should know."

With those words, the deputy turned and walked away. After he walked out Terry stood in the door, and watched him get in his car and drive away. While he hated to admit it, his words had shaken him. The discussion about his father had made old feelings resurface-feelings of hurt and resentment. Everyone had thought his father was such a great man, and yet he had been gone most of the time helping others while his wife and son were left alone. At an early age, Terry had learned that he had to rely on himself if he wanted to be successful in the world. Luckily he had discovered the one thing he was better at than anybody else - playing football. That had been his ticket to freedom, and to all the things he wanted - money, fame, and independence. Yet now it seemed that all of those things had not brought him the happiness he wanted. His wife had left him, his mother was always angry with him, he was attacked by the press, and his coach had just suspended him. The only person in his life who loved and respected him was his son.

He thought of Mr. Powell. The man had been unreasonable and demanding, but he guessed he could understand his situation. Still, there was nothing more he could do.

He soon closed the door and went back to watching the films, trying to put everything that had happened in the past couple of days out of his mind.

At two-thirty, he got in his car and drove to the school to pick up his son. As always, Jacob was excited to see him.

"How was school today, Son?"

"It was okay, I guess."

"You guess? You don't know?"

"Most of it was okay, but I got in an argument with Joseph."

"You and him are best friends. What did you argue about?"

"Well, he said you shouldn't have kicked the other player yesterday, and I told him he didn't know what he was talking about."

"Really?"

"Yep. I told him you were the best receiver to ever play football, and you could do whatever you wanted."

"Oh, really? And what did he say about that?"

"He said I was a jerk, and he didn't want to be friends anymore. I don't care, Dad. He's not good enough for us anyway, huh?"

Terry didn't answer, but gave his son a sad smile. The rest of the ride home was uncomfortable and quiet. After getting out of the car, Terry put his hand on his son's shoulder, and the two walked into the house.

"Jacob," said Terry, "I need you to help me do something."

"Sure, Dad. What?"

"I have to make a phone call first, but I want you to go into your room and put on some old clothes."

"Okay. What are we going to do?"

"I'll show you in a few minutes."

His son walked toward his room, while Terry went into the den and picked up the phone. His coach answered on the second ring.

"Hey, Coach," said Terry.

"Hi, Terry," said coach Dillon. "How's it going?"

"It's fine, Coach. Look, I'll get to the point. I just called to say

I'm sorry?"

"You're sorry? For what?"

"For what happened yesterday, and for being such a jerk. I just want you to know when I come back you won't have any more problems with me."

"Really. What brought this on?'

"Let's just say I have a new spirit."

Terry hung up the phone and walked to his son's room. Jacob had just finished changing into old clothes.

"So, what are we doing, Dad?

"Well, while I'm off, I need to keep in shape, so I thought I would move that fence out back. It's always been kind of crooked, and I think it's time it's straightened."

"Okay, Dad."

"And one other thing, Jacob."

"What's that, Dad?"

"I think we need to find a way for you to spend more time with your mother."

The two went into the garage and removed their tools, then walked into the back yard, enjoying the view of the valley below.

AUTHOR'S COMMENTS

The Greatest Gift is a collection of short stories which deal with people in difficult situations who try to solve their problems on their own before looking to God for direction. While the stories are all fiction, I have tried to deal with realistic life situations, IE, marriage, finance, forgiveness, etc., which we all face at one time or another. It is my belief that all of life's problems are addressed in the Bible. While I am not a minister or theologian, I have spent much time reading and studying the Bible as well other Christian writers, so hopefully my stories are Biblically sound. I hope you enjoy them.

Sincerely,
Larry Buttram

Other books by Larry Buttram

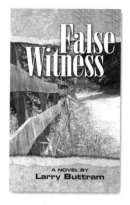

FALSE WITNESS

It is the summer of 1963 in rural East Tennessee. Ethan Ward, thirteen, is enjoying his summer vacation. On a trip to a friend's house--on a hot and dusty country road--he sees two black strangers shoot and kill a Deputy Sheriff. They escape leaving him the only witness. The men are never caught, and for years Ethan lives in fear of their return. Then, in a chance meeting six years later, he learns that things are not always what they appear, and that good and evil aren't divided along the color line.

HONOR THY SISTER

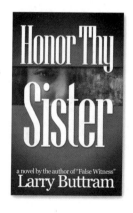

It is 1978 in Murfreesboro, Tennessee, and Sally Ward, with a caring husband, two young children, and a fulfilling job as a teacher, is content with her life. Then, her wayward sister, Merita, moves back home, and her world is torn apart. Merita, or Rita as she now likes to be called, apologizes for her past behavior, and for abandoning the family. Sally accepts her apology, and is happy to have her sister back in her life. Then, when disaster strikes, Sally must decide if she believes her sister was an innocent victim, or was the cause of the tragedy.